CFU

This book should be returned to any branch of the
Lancashire County Library on or before the date shown

SÉANCE OF TERROR

Chalmers decides to attend one of Dr. Lanson's nightly séances because it's somewhere warm to rest his weary feet. A decision he regrets when a luminous cloud forms above the assembled people. Strangely, from the cloud comes a warning: someone there is about to die to prevent them from revealing secrets. A man defiantly leaps to his feet, the lights are extinguished, the man's voice is cut off and an ear-piercing shriek reverberates around the room . . .

SYDNEY J. BOUNDS

SÉANCE OF TERROR

Complete and Unabridged

LINFORD
Leicester

First published in Great Britain

First Linford Edition
published 2013

British Library CIP Data

Bounds, Sydney J.
  Séance of terror.- -(Linford mystery library)
  1. Detective and mystery stories.
  2. Large type books.
  I. Title II. Series
  823.9'14–dc23

  ISBN 978–1–4448–1436–1

11814667
Published by
F. A. Thorpe (Publishing)
Anstey, Leicestershire

Set by Words & Graphics Ltd.
Anstey, Leicestershire
Printed and bound in Great Britain by
T. J. International Ltd., Padstow, Cornwall

This book is printed on acid-free paper

1

Séance of Terror

1

Voice from the Dead

It was one of those nights when even a cadaver feels chilled to the bone. A raw-cold mist swirled in from the sea, swallowing Manhattan Island in a grey shroud.

Down on the East Side, Burt Chalmers shrugged a thin jacket tighter about his broad shoulders. There were fifty cents in his pocket, a lethargy in the way he dragged his huge body along the sidewalk, and no hope in his heart.

The dismal wail of a tug's hooter echoed through the mist, reminding him of the nearness of the Hudson River. The Hudson, with its ice-cold waters, bleak and comfortless — but so final. How many derelicts of Life's relentless progress had ended up in those black waters?

You either went on — or under. Life — or Death. It was so easy, so tempting.

You let the icy chill freeze your body, let the dank waters slide smoothly over your head. Then it was all over. No more fighting, no more living — no more loving. Abruptly, Burt Chalmers pushed the idea out of his head. He shuddered and turned away.

A red light winked at him through the greyness. A building loomed ahead. He followed the brownstone wall till he came to the doorway. Over the porch, a red neon sign flickered luridly. He stopped to read the sign.

DR. LANSON — MEDIUM
Séances nightly — all welcome.

Chalmers laughed wolfishly. Just another racket to clean out the suckers. Mumbo-jumbo and stage magic — and Dr. Lanson raked in the greenbacks.

He was about to pass on when the idea struck him. Why not take advantage of Dr. Lanson's hospitality? All welcome, the sign said. And he was cold and footsore — past caring where his next meal or the night's lodging came from.

He stared blindly into the damp mist eddying around the house. He heard a car go past, but the mist was now so thick he couldn't even make out the highlights. He shivered, looked in at the open doorway — at least it would be warm in there. And he could take the weight off his feet.

There were two steps up to the porch. Then a short passage and a flight of wooden stairs. There was no carpet on the stairs and his heavy feet echoed eerily on the bare boards. At the top of the stairs a closed door bore the notice:

Please Walk In.

'Said the Spider to the Fly!' he murmured, pushing open the door.

His first impression was that he had wandered on to the set of a Hollywood epic — Oriental style.

The floor was thickly carpeted, the walls hung with bizarre tapestries. There was a half-circle of chairs, about two-thirds of them filled with people. Chalmers sank easily into the nearest that was empty.

In the centre, a thin-faced man with a pointed beard and pince-nez was mumbling an incantation over a brazier. The brazier glowed redly, the only illumination in the room. Incense burned in bronze chalices, filling the room with a pungent sweetness.

Chalmers dozed. The room was warm, the air heavy with the sickly incense. He nodded — caught himself as he almost rolled off the chair. He looked around, studying the faces of the people intent on the man over the brazier.

A mixed lot. One white-haired lady from the West Side, overburdened with jewellery. A lamb to the slaughter. A middle-class wife who had dragged along her bored husband. Wrinkled faces, bright eyes in dead faces, the faces of people living on after life had gone. Waiting the call from beyond the grave.

Chalmers felt sorry for them. At least he hadn't reached that stage yet. Then he saw the girl. He straightened in his seat to get a better look at her.

She was young. Nineteen, maybe twenty. And beautiful. Her figure was the sort you pay big money on Broadway just to look at. She had black hair, falling down over smooth shoulders. The dark oval of her face was tinted redly by the glowing coals in the brazier. Wide, dark eyes watched the man performing the incantation.

When she looked up, Chalmers saw that the pupils of her eyes were dilated with fear. Her lips moved soundlessly. Her fingers beat an uneasy tattoo on her knee. Her fear communicated itself to him. He shivered and looked away. What was the girl afraid of?

He watched her out of the corner of his eye. Her hand strayed to the man next to her. She gripped his wrist till it gleamed whitely in the firelight. Chalmers saw him glance at her, pat her hand as if to reassure her.

Chalmers wished it were he doing the reassuring. She was sure a cute number, Then he remembered Joyce —

He scowled and looked away. But the feeling persisted. This beautiful young girl was frightened — badly frightened. And Chalmers wanted to do something about it.

He wondered who the man was sitting next to her. He studied him carefully. A thin man, well-dressed, with a pale face and blue eyes. He wondered if the man were her fiancé. A glance at the engagement ring on the girl's finger confirmed this possibility. But what was either of them doing at this pseudo-fetish?

The man, Chalmers saw, was all tensed up. Not frightened like the girl, but taut. Taut as a bowstring. His face showed plainly that he was waiting for something to happen. What was he waiting for? The same thing that frightened the girl?

Chalmers let his eyes wander to the man by the brazier. Dr. Lanson? A long robe, decorated with crescents and interlocked triangles, dropped to his ankles. His feet were covered by thin moccasins, his head by a turban from which a large ruby glittered.

As he chanted sibilant runes, Dr. Lanson's slim white fingers cast a powder onto the glowing coals. The powder burnt blood-red, filling the room with the overpowering smell of a musky perfume. The atmosphere thickened. Chalmers felt his breath catch on the pungent empyreuma.

Dr. Lanson's assistant stood in the shadows behind him. Chalmers hadn't noticed him before, so still and silent was he. A small man with a red, wrinkled face and gnarled hands. The right hand twitched and Chalmers saw that the small finger was missing.

Three Fingers wore a chocolate coat with a chocolate tie against a white shirt. His shoes were white with chocolate-brown toe-caps. A cloth cap was pulled down over his forehead so that his eyes were covered.

Chalmers' attention was suddenly jerked back to Dr. Lanson. The medium had ceased his incantation. Now he stood upright, arms outstretched above his head. Bright, piercing eyes glittered behind the pince-nez and his short, pointed beard jutted out like the finger of an avenging devil. He spoke in a loud, clear voice that carried to every corner of the room.

'Ai! Ai! In the name of the Horned One, the Shadow that blots out all Light, the Toad spawning in the darkness beyond the Universe, I command thee — Belchior, spirit messenger from the Other life beyond the veil of Death — come forth!'

In the moment of awful silence that

9

followed Dr. Lanson's pronouncement, Chalmers felt his body go rigid. The hairs on the nape of his neck stiffened. Sweat broke out on his forehead.

He forced himself to relax. Mumbo-jumbo and stage magic. Nothing to it. It was the setting, the red glow of coals in the brazier, the thick carpets and curtains, the sickly smell of incense that got him. Nothing else.

He glanced at the other people in the room. Without exception, they strained forward in their seats, expectantly, hopefully. The girl's face was white. A tiny trickle of blood oozed down her chin as she bit her lip. The man beside her seemed to be in a trance — his face ashen . . .

Chalmers started. A luminous cloud formed in the air over the heads of the assembled people. It swirled mistily, an eerie blue light emanating from the centre of the cloud. Chalmers' lip curled. How could anyone be taken in so easily? A luminous gas released from a vent in the wall.

A voice spoke out of the cloud. A

curiously flat voice, as if it had travelled a long way and lost its resonance on the journey. Ventriloquism. Chalmers watched Three Fingers to see if he could detect the assistant's mouth moving. But Three Fingers was too far back, too much in the shadow to tell.

The flat voice from the cloud said:

'I am here, O Master. What is your wish?'

Dr. Lanson's clear tones rang through the room.

'There are those here who would speak with one who has passed the barrier. Is there one to answer?'

The silence that came was almost tangible. It was heavy, oppressive. It seemed that everyone had stopped breathing. Chalmers forced himself to expel the air from his lungs. The sound was like a balloon deflating.

The voice from the eerie blue cloud came again:

'There is one here who would speak with someone on the other side — '

The gathering craned forward. White faces gleamed in the red light of the coals.

Chalmers felt himself carried with them. He, too, felt the wave of tension surge through the room. The voice might be a trick — he told himself it must be a trick — but in that incense-perfumed murk it was strangely convincing.

A second voice strained through the luminous cloud. It was high-pitched, with an odd rhythm to it — a sing-song chanting that seemed to race ahead of the words. Chalmers watched Three Fingers' face but his lips were in shadow. It was impossible to tell if he was the owner of the voice.

'I speak to one in the room on the other side,' chanted the sing-song voice. 'It is a man. He is in great danger. The scythe of the Grim Reaper swings above his head. The Sands of Time run low. I see the bony skull of Death grinning over his shoulder — '

A coldness seemed to seep into the room. A shudder ran through the crowd. Chalmers felt his flesh crawl. The high-pitched voice sang on:

'A warning to this man. Let him heed the voices of his advisers. Silence is demanded if he is to avert the threat hanging over him. Silence. A man with secrets needs be a man without a tongue — '

Too many things happened in a hurry for Chalmers ever to sort out their order of occurrence.

As the chanting died away, the eerie cloud seemed to lose its luminosity and disperse. The man with the pale face and blue eyes, next to the girl, leapt to his feet.

'You can't frighten me!' he cried, half-sobbing. 'I know your game — I won't keep quiet — '

Chalmers' eyes flicked from the dead-white face of the girl to Dr. Lanson. The medium's hands hovered over the brazier. A fine powder dropped from his sleeves onto the glowing coals. Abruptly, the coals spluttered and went out, plunging the room into darkness.

The man's voice was cut off.

Chalmers froze in his seat as the girl's ear-piercing shriek reverberated through the room.

2

The Lady is Frightened

Burt Chalmers came out of his seat like a shot from a catapult. He rocketed across the room in the direction of the girl, knocking chairs flying in the dark. He heard a grunt as he collided with someone, staggered and lost his sense of direction.

He lost seconds fumbling in his pocket for a match struck it impatiently. The yellow flare revealed the girl's taut figure. She was standing upright, rigid, one hand over her mouth to choke the scream swelling in her throat.

He dropped a hand on her shoulder.

'What — ' he began.

Her painted nails clawed at his face She made a strange noise, half scream, half sob. She turned, struck at Chalmers again and fled across the room to the door.

He staggered back under her blow.

Scared as Hell, he thought. What had frightened her in the dark? He wiped his stinging face where her hand had struck him. His hand came away wet. He rubbed his fingers together, smelt them. Blood! His face wasn't cut — so it must have come from her hand as she hit him.

The girl had reached the door and jerked it open. The lamp in the hall at the top of the stairs shone faint beams into the room. Chalmers glimpsed the startled people milling around him. Dr. Lanson was still standing over the brazier, but of Three Fingers there was no sign.

Suddenly he remembered the man who had been with the girl — the man who had been warned by the phoney voice from the grave. Where was he? Chalmers was prepared to swear that no one except the girl had left through the door. His eyes swept round the room without alighting on the man he sought.

He caught sight of some red spots on the carpet, between the chairs where the girl and her fiancé had been sitting. He knelt down and smeared the spots with his fingers. Blood!

Chalmers rose to his feet. His lips set in a grim line. Murder! But the corpse had disappeared — and so had Three Fingers. And the girl was scared and running wild in New York's East Side. If Chalmer's suspicions were correct, she was in grave danger.

Ignoring the chatter of the people around him, Chalmers crossed to the door and clattered noisily down the stairs after the girl.

The red neon sign still invited all to the nightly séance held by Dr. Lanson and the mist still swirled greyly about the brownstone house. He paused on the steps, trying to decide which way she had gone. He strained his ears, heard the faint clicking of high heels on the sidewalk and hurried off towards the sound.

He ran fast, letting his long legs carry his bulk in easy, loping strides. The mist thinned a little at the end of the block and he caught a glimpse of the girl as she darted across the road under the yellow light of a street-lamp.

She looked round, her face white, and started running again. Hell, Chalmers thought, she's heard me — and thinks I'm one of the gang after her. He lengthened his stride, quickened his pace.

He caught her at the next intersection. She was out of breath and leaning heavily against the street-lamp. Chalmers put his arms round her to keep her hands out of his face.

'Now take it easy, lady,' he said smoothly. 'I'm not going to hurt you. I guess you're in bad trouble and if there's anything I can do to help, you've only to say so. At least, allow me to escort you home.'

Her reaction caught him unawares. She flung her arms round his neck, buried her face in his chest and burst into tears.

'They murdered him!' she sobbed. 'They'll kill me next — oh, don't let them get me — save me — please . . .'

Chalmers soothed her gently. Poor kid, she'd had a tough time. Scared out of her wits. Living on her nerve and now it's gone. His rough hands caressed her.

'Now don't worry,' he said quietly. 'No one's going to hurt you while Burt Chalmers is around. Dry your eyes and

I'll see you safely home.'

She lifted her face to him and tried to smile.

'Thank you,' she said. 'I'll be all right now.'

Chalmers looked down at her. His mouth went dry and he felt his pulse quicken as he held her close. God, she was beautiful!

The yellow street-light showed high cheekbones and wide, appealing eyes. Her lips were full and very red. He wanted to crush his mouth over hers . . .

She was wearing a dark-red dress that moulded itself to her young curves. Her legs were long and slim and encased in sheer silk hose.

Chalmers pushed her away from him.

'Where to?' he asked abruptly.

She gave an address a dozen blocks away and Burt put his arm around her slim waist and piloted her through the mist. She didn't speak on the way to her home and he respected her silence. When they arrived at the apartment house where she lived, she invited him inside.

'A drink?' she suggested.

Chalmers said, laconically: 'Beer.'

She smiled faintly.

'There's only brandy, I'm afraid.'

He nodded briefly.

'Please sit down,' she said, indicating the straight-backed sofa along one wall.

Chalmers sat down. The girl poured two brandies, passed him one, and sat down beside him. She emptied her glass in one gulp and refilled it. Chalmers sipped his slowly, letting the fiery liquid roll around his tongue, warming him.

He was aware that her eyes were on him, puzzling over his derelict appearance, wondering how far she could trust him.

Chalmers smoothed his blond hair back with a broad hand, ran his fingers round the stubble of his chin. He wished he had shaved that morning.

'You look like a down and out,' she said critically, 'but then again — you don't, if you get what I mean.'

Chalmers drained the brandy from his glass and turned grey eyes on her. He waved a large hand casually.

'It's not a new story,' he said. His smile

19

was bitter. 'I was in the U.S. Marines — sergeant — and I fell for a good-looking dame. Fell like a log. I worshipped the very ground she walked on. Nothing was too good for her.'

He fell silent, reliving the past. Quietly, the girl refilled his glass. He sipped appreciatively and went on:

'We were married and I got my discharge. We were going to buy a little place in the country — up in Maine — and settle down to raise a family. I was held up by a lot of red tape and she persuaded me to make all my savings over to her so she could go right ahead and fix things up for when I got out. It was one swell idea — for her! Of course, I didn't see her again — nor my money. I was just another sucker taken for a ride. So I ended up flat broke, out of a job and out of the Marines. To make everything perfect, I found out she already had a husband — so I wasn't even married!'

The girl's dark eyes were soft and pitying.

'That's a bad deal. I figure a guy like you deserves something better than a run-around. What's your name?'

'Chalmers. My friends call me Burt.'

'I'm Ann, Burt. Ann Stevens. I'm in terrible trouble. I think they're going to murder me.'

Burt took her hand in his.

'No one's going to murder you if I can stop them,' he said softly. 'Suppose you tell me what it's all about?'

Ann looked at him in silence. Her raven-black hair fell down over slim shoulders and Chalmers caught a whiff of exotic perfume. He had to fight to control himself. He wanted to grab her and kiss her — but he knew if he tried anything like that with this girl, everything would be over between them. And he wanted their friendship to develop.

At last, she made up her mind.

'I believe I can trust you, Burt,' she said, 'and God knows, I need someone I can trust. It's not such a simple story as yours and I don't have all the pieces of the puzzle yet. I only know that Dudley was murdered in that horrible room back there — and I'm in terrible danger.'

She pulled out a cigarette case and

offered it to Burt. He took one and lit it gratefully. It tasted good — he hadn't smoked in three days.

'Dudley was the man you were with at the séance?' he queried. 'Your fiancé?'

Ann nodded, drawing on her cigarette and blowing a smoke ring. She watched the ring rise slowly to the ceiling.

'Yes,' she agreed, 'Dudley Brooks and I were engaged to be married. The wedding was to have been next month.'

Burt said, trying hard to sound as if he meant it:

'I'm sorry.'

Ann shrugged.

'It's all over now,' she said fatalistically. Her voice was perfectly calm. 'It was through Dudley that I first met Dr. Lanson and the people who go to his séances.'

She shuddered and inhaled deeply on the cigarette.

'I had known Dudley all my life. We went to the same school and grew up together. It was tacitly assumed by our families that eventually we would marry — but I never really loved him.'

Burt felt a lot better hearing that. He didn't like the idea of stealing a dead man's love. But that confession made it all right.

'Dudley was very interested in the occult. I suppose you'd call him a student of the occult. He used to go to séances and investigate different forms of black magic. He has a library at home filled with all kinds of books dealing with sorcery and the Black Arts.'

'You mean he took that kind of thing seriously?' Chalmers interrupted, a look of incredulous wonder on his rugged face. 'It stuck out a mile back there that Dr. Lanson was a phoney. A cloud of gas and a ventriloquist throwing his voice and all the old dames lapping up the message from the other side!'

'Oh, Dudley knew there was a lot of faking connected with mediums and their powers, but he believed that one or two of them really did have some strange power that other people haven't got. And it was in hope of contacting the few genuine mediums that he investigated every séance he could.'

Ann paused to stub out her cigarette in the china ashtray on the small table beside the sofa.

'Another brandy?' she suggested.

Burt shook his head.

'Not for me — I know when to stop.'

She smiled and continued her story:

'When Dudley first met Dr. Lanson, he was quite sure he was a fake — but he couldn't prove it. So he went to his séances regularly in the hope of getting proof. Well, one day he found out that the séances were only a blind for a bigger racket. He was very worried about this but wouldn't tell me what he had learnt. I know he was scared about it and considered that Dr. Lanson should be exposed and he tried to make me keep out of it. But I couldn't let him face whatever it was alone, so I went with him as often as I could.'

'Did you get any kind of line on what it was he discovered?' Chalmers asked.

Ann hesitated, then shook her head.

'No — except that it concerned what Dudley called Dr. Lanson's Inner Circle. I got the impression they meet once a month — but not at the place we were at tonight. I don't know where.'

Chalmers considered what Ann had told him.

'It boils down to this, then. Dudley found out something about Dr. Lanson that automatically made him a candidate for a coffin — and because you've been around with him, you're in danger of the same treatment. You could go to the police — but your story's too thin for official recognition. Dudley disappeared — we can't produce the body. You can bet Dr. Lanson has cleaned the bloodstains off the carpet by now. I can corroborate your statement but it's hardly likely the police will take any notice of an out-of-work bum. Meanwhile, you're liable to turn up in the Hudson with your throat cut.'

Ann shuddered.

'What am I going to do?' she asked.

Chalmers' grey eyes regarded her levelly.

'If you feel you can trust me, Ann,' he said, 'I'd like to stick around and look after you.'

She gave him her hand. Chalmers pressed it warmly.

'I do trust you, Burt — and I'd really like to have you around.'

'That's a deal,' he said.

'It's late now,' Ann said, 'what are you going to do? Will you stop here?'

She blushed as she realised what she had said.

'I mean,' she ran on hurriedly, 'you can sleep on the couch here.'

Chalmers grinned.

'That'll do me.'

Ann quickly made up a bed on the couch.

'I'll sleep easier knowing you're out here,' she said.

She looked at him from lowered eyelashes. Her lips parted in a smile — then she skipped across the room and kissed him lightly on the mouth.

'Good night, Burt,' she said softly, and turned and ducked into the bedroom.

Chalmers stood motionless, staring after her slim young figure. He grinned. Then the key turned in the lock and he was alone in the room.

3

Three Fingers Again

Chalmers lay on the couch in the dark. He listened to the loud ticking of the clock over the mantelpiece and the light breathing of the girl in the room next door.

The clock struck twice. Two a.m. Chalmers shifted the pillow under his head and turned over. His grey eyes were wide and he had never felt less sleepy in his life.

He rubbed thoughtfully at the stubble of blond hair coating his jaw and wondered if he was making a fool of himself again. When he remembered Joyce, the curvaceous armful who had skipped with his savings, he felt a bitter distrust of all females.

And here he was, playing knight in armour to Ann's damsel in distress. A smile flickered briefly about his lips and went out. The stakes were higher this time. If he lost out now, he'd end up with the worms in the graveyard.

He considered the idea of getting to his feet and walking out. He owed the girl nothing — why should he stick his neck out for her? But the more he thought about her, the more certain he became that he'd never leave her to the mercy of Dr. Lanson and his killers.

The taste of her goodnight kiss still lingered about his lips — and it was a flavour he wanted to experience again. And her dark eyes had held the promise of more intimate favours to come if he got her out of this jam . . .

A soft click at the door alerted him. He rolled off the couch and dropped softly on the balls of his stockinged feet. The noise was repeated some minutes later. Chalmers crouched down behind the sofa, straining his eyes in the dark, watching the door.

He guessed that someone was trying to pick the lock. There was a gentle thud as the key was pushed out of the lock to drop on the mat inside. Then, a louder click as the tumblers snapped back. The door opened quietly and a black shadow glided into the room.

A torch beam flicked round the room. Chalmers ducked hastily as the beam of light played over the couch — but the glimpse he'd had was sufficient to identify the intruder. It was Three Fingers, Dr. Lanson's assistant.

The torchlight snapped off and Three Fingers moved silently towards the door of Ann's bedroom. Chalmers let him go to work on the lock before he moved, then he stepped from cover and crept up on him.

His intention had been to take his quarry from behind, banking on the element of surprise to offset the advantage of any weapon the other might have. But his luck was out. Even as Chalmers tensed himself to grapple with his opponent, Three Fingers, alarmed by some slight sound, turned sideways.

Chalmers' hands, which should have gone round Three Fingers' throat, thudded harmlessly against the man's body as he straightened up.

Snarling, Three Fingers dropped his torch and snatched out a glittering ice pick. Chalmers dropped flat as the point of the ice pick buried itself in the woodwork over his head. He didn't need telling how Dudley Brooks had been silenced so efficiently at the séance.

Three Fingers followed up his attack by flinging himself at Chalmers, wrapping his arms about him. Chalmers threw himself backwards onto the floor, carrying Three Fingers with him and breaking his hold.

Despite his extra height and weight, Chalmers found his opponent a slippery customer. The smaller man wriggled like an eel, twisting and lunging viciously with his fists. They rolled across the room, locked in deadly embrace, each trying to finish the other in one swift killing blow.

Chalmers got his hands round Three Fingers' throat. He started squeezing — staggered back with a cry of agony as he received a knee in the groin. He lay writhing on the floor, his eyes blinded by a flood of tears, while Three Fingers prepared to administer the death punch.

He heard a door open and the light clicked on. Ann Stevens, alarmed by the sound of fighting in the next room, had come out to see what was happening. Three Fingers turned his attention to her — unconsciously extending Chalmers' lease of life.

'Get away, Ann!' Chalmers croaked desperately. 'Leave him to me!'

He climbed to his feet, ignoring the stabbing pain in his groin, and threw himself bodily at Three Fingers. He bore the killer to the floor and rolled atop him, slugging heavy punches to the smaller man's body.

Three Fingers wriggled clear — swung a short jab to Chalmers' solar plexus that stopped him cold. Chalmers swayed on his feet. Sweat ran down his face and into his mouth. It had a salty tang.

He crouched low, covering his body with his arms as Three Fingers came in, swinging lefts and rights with telling force. He grabbed Three Fingers in a bear hug — his arms tightened. The air squeezed out of Three Fingers' lungs. Chalmers exerted all his force . . .

'Let him go,' Ann's voice said from behind him, 'I've got him covered.'

Chalmers released the killer and stepped back. Too late he heard Ann say:

'It's a trick, Burt — watch out!'

As Three Fingers lunged forward, Chalmers saw that Ann was completely unarmed. In the brief span of time that it took the smaller man's arm to swing in a vicious arc, he remembered that Three Fingers was a ventriloquist — it had been Dr. Lanson's assistant, mimicking Ann's voice, who had spoken.

Chalmers realised that too late. It seemed as if a hand grenade exploded in his face. He felt himself falling — a dark pool opened up to engulf him — then nothingness . . .

*   *   *

A harsh light beat down into his eyes. His head throbbed like a power-crazy dynamo. His ears registered a confused blur of sound, which, as consciousness slowly returned, he identified as the jazzed-up pounding of his heart.

The floor beneath him was hard and unyielding. He tried to move his body — and his muscles shrieked agonizing protests. He let his mind sink back into semi-consciousness. The pain eased a little.

After a time he began to wonder who he was: and where he was; and how he had gotten into such a mess. He tried to solve the problem by thinking it out — but no solution came.

He decided it could be no more uncomfortable to stand up than it was to lie heaped up on bone-bruising boards. Ignoring the pain, he lifted himself and clung to the mantelpiece.

A clock ticked ominously in his face. The hands stood at 2.25. He wondered whether it was a.m. or p.m. The glass over the mantelpiece showed a battered face, grey eyes, a stubble round the chin and a tangle of blond hair. It looked familiar.

He licked his lips and tasted salt. His nose had been bleeding and the blood had run down into his mouth.

His first conscious memory was of Joyce. She must have hit him in the mouth with a flat-iron. But why should she do that? Hadn't she done enough to him already?

He was bitterly cursing all females when his eyes rested on the photograph of the girl with dark hair and deep black eyes. The photograph was standing in a metal frame on the mantelpiece beside the clock. And again the face seemed familiar. He read the name underneath: Ann Stevens.

And suddenly it all came back.

He remembered taking her home. And Three Fingers. There had been a fight. Then Ann came out of her bedroom — she had hastily thrown a dressing gown over silk pyjamas, but he still remembered admiring the perfection of her young figure before Three Fingers hit him for the last time.

Desperately, he called:

'Ann! Ann! Where are you, Ann?'

He searched the apartment, but he knew it was no good. Ann Stevens had disappeared. Fine watchdog you are, Burt Chalmers! What was he going to do now?

He looked at the clock, and this time it

meant something. Half-an-hour had elapsed since Three Fingers had arrived, Time enough for him to get clean away — and there was no doubt that he had taken the girl with him.

The light was still on. He crossed to the window and peered out. The gray mist hung like a death shroud over Manhattan. No hope of tracing anyone in that.

Apparently, no one had been roused by the sound of the fight — or if they had, they had very prudently decided to mind their own business.

He searched the flat, pocketed some loose change Ann had left on the table. The ice pick that had so nearly ended his career was still sticking in the door frame. He pulled it out and slipped it in his pocket. Quietly he left the apartment. Burt Chalmers badly wanted to meet Three Fingers again — there was something he had to settle with him . . .

4

The Inner Circle

The police gave him a rough time. Of course, the Captain had eyed him with suspicion as soon as he entered the Homicide Bureau. His face was a mess; he hadn't shaved for three days; his coat was torn and he looked like any other East Side bum.

The Captain listened to his story with the bored air of one who has heard it all before. Then he held him in the cooler while the night sergeant checked to see if the girl had disappeared. When he found out she had, the Captain gave him a going-over.

Finally, the police got around to Dr. Lanson's place. But the bare walls told them nothing. The doctor and his assistant had left in a hurry.

The Captain scratched his head and said it was up to the Missing Persons

Bureau. Then they slung him out on the sidewalk because they couldn't cook up a charge to hold him any longer.

Burt Chalmers pounded East Side looking for Ann — or Dr. Lanson, or Three Fingers, or anyone who could give him a lead on the girl. Two days had passed since she had been taken from under his very nose. Two days, which Chalmers had spent asking questions of the people neighbouring the house where the séances had been held; two days wearing out shoe-leather, hunting clues.

Maybe it had been a mistake to go to the police. If he hadn't wasted time perhaps he could have picked up the trail while it was still warm. But he figured it was a police job — apparently the cops thought otherwise.

And, by now, Ann might be dead. His mouth tightened in a thin line. If Dr. Lanson and Three Fingers had murdered her, he'd never rest until he'd evened the score. The ache in his heart told him how much the girl meant to him. He had to find her. But how?

He had exhausted all the possibilities

he could think up. Dr. Lanson seemed to have disappeared into thin air — and New York was a big city to search. Assuming he was still in New York.

He turned into a drugstore for a coffee and sandwich. The sandwich was like sawdust in his mouth; the coffee tasteless. There was a paper lying on the tabletop. Idly he scanned the headlines to see if the police had discovered anything.

A murder at a nightspot. Baseball scores. Rioting in the South. He turned the pages disinterestedly, bitterly. What use paying a police force if they didn't do anything about Ann? The pages became a blur. He found the coffee had gone cold and he was down to the personal column. Two words caught his eye — *inner circle*.

Chalmers almost dropped the cup. The Inner Circle! That was the name Ann had given to the coterie on the inside of Dr. Lanson's racket. Eagerly, he read the notice:

The Inner Circle meets tonight at 11.30.

That was all. No name. No rendezvous. He read it through three times, seeking for some hidden meaning. Did the notice concern Dr. Lanson or was it merely the meeting of some quite innocuous society? Would the doctor have the nerve to insert a notice in the press, telling everyone who cared to read it, when he was holding his next meeting?

Chalmers considered the point carefully. Why not? The notice wouldn't mean a thing to anyone not in the doctor's confidence. The more he thought about it, the more likely it seemed that it was a clue to Dr. Lanson — and through him, to Ann.

He lit a cigarette and tried to plan a course of action. It told him when the meeting was to be held, but not the more important factor — where. Of course. The members of the Inner Circle would know that. But Chalmers didn't.

A notice in the personal column. Someone would have to insert and pay for that. Who? Dr. Lanson? At least, someone in touch with him.

Chalmers shot across to the phone booth and jammed a nickel in the slot. He dialled the newspaper offices and got the department handling the personal ads.

A bored voice said:

'Can I help you?'

Chalmers poured syrup into his voice. He had to know the answer to his question.

'I'm ringing about an ad in today's paper,' he said. 'It gives the time of meeting of the Inner Circle, but unfortunately I've lost the address. If you could give me the address or the phone number of the person who inserted the ad, I could find out from them.'

'Hold the line — I'll check back.'

Chalmers waited in a sweat. It seemed a couple of weeks before the bored voice came back on the line.

'The ad was inserted by a Mr. Rivers. The address is 1116, East 47th Street. No phone number.'

'Thanks — thanks a lot.'

Chalmers jammed the receiver back on its rest with a sigh of relief. He had something to work on now. He ordered another coffee — it tasted like nectar this time — and sat down to plan his next step.

Call in the police? Not after the way they had treated him the last time. No, he'd handle this his own way. But, for Ann's sake, he couldn't afford to fail. He had no idea what sort of opposition he'd be up against. Dr. Lanson and Three Fingers, at least. And the mysterious Mr. Rivers. He needed a weapon. The police had taken the ice pick off him when they searched him, at the station — a pity that — he'd dearly love to return that to Three Fingers.

A gun was the obvious thing. But he didn't possess one, and — even including the loose change he had picked up at Ann's flat — he didn't have the money to buy one. Then there was the slight matter of a licence.

Well, there were other ways.

Chalmers got up and walked out of the drugstore. He walked around till he found a second-hand shop with a Colt .45 for sale. Then he walked around till closing time.

Five minutes before the shop was due to close, he walked in and up to the counter.

'Nice Colt you've got in the window,' he said casually. 'What's the price tag?'

The proprietor beamed at him.

'It's in good condition,' he said, 'nice action, cheap too — only twenty-five bucks. O.K.?'

'I'll take a closer look.'

'Sure.'

The proprietor hurried to the window, took the gun out of its case and wiped the oil off it. He handed it to Chalmers for inspection.

Burt tried the action, lined up the sights. It was a nice job. Just what he wanted.

'Can you load it?'

'Sure — you gotta licence?'

'Yeah.'

Chalmers took out his wallet and rifled through some papers, searching for an imaginary licence. The proprietor finished loading the chambers and put the gun down on the counter.

'I'll take a box of shells, too,' Chalmers said.

The proprietor turned to get a box from the rack behind him. When he turned round again, he was facing a loaded Colt.

'No noise — no trouble!' Chalmers said grimly. He reached across, grabbed the box of shells and stuck them in his pocket.

He yanked the telephone cable apart. He didn't want the cops on his trail as soon as he left the shop.

'You won't get far,' the proprietor said.

'I'll take a chance. If you want to take a chance too — just stick your head out of the door and start yelling. I may be waiting around outside.'

Keeping the shop proprietor covered, Chalmers backed over to the door. He ducked outside and started running, shoving the Colt out of sight in his pocket. He dived down the first subway entrance and took the first train out of the area. Then he doubled back and crossed his tracks.

He felt a lot better with the comforting bulge of a .45 in his pocket. Next stop 1116, East 47th, the Inner Circle and Dr. Lanson. Then Ann . . .

The residence of Mr. Rivers was a

faded brick building with no pretence to cleanliness. It had a short flight of steps up to a wide porch. The door was solid with a heavy brass knocker.

Chalmers didn't use the knocker. He found himself a shadowy doorway opposite and settled down to wait.

It was just on eleven and a light in an upstairs window informed him that Mr. Rivers had not yet left for the meeting of the Inner Circle. The mist began to drift in from the sea. It swirled lazily round the doorway where Chalmers waited, hiding him from passing eyes.

A nearby clock struck eleven. As the last stroke reverberated on the clammy air, a cab drew up outside No. 1116. Chalmers tensed as the upstairs light blinked out. This was it. Rivers was about to leave for the meeting place.

He ducked across the road and spreadeagled himself across the luggage rack. He heard footsteps clatter down the stone steps, a mutter of voices, a door slam, then the cab moved off.

Cautiously Chalmers raised himself to look through the rear window. The shock of identifying the passenger almost caused him to lose his hold. The mysterious Mr. Rivers was none other than his old antagonist — Three Fingers!

Chalmers eased himself back onto the luggage rack. His breath came quicker. So his hunch had been right — and he was heading for Dr. Lanson's Inner Circle — and Ann.

The cab headed downtown. It was difficult to pick out the route in the grey mist, but the hooting of tugs told him they were near the river. The cab swung off the main thoroughfare and picked a devious route through twisting back streets.

As the clock struck the half-hour, the cab swung into the curb and stopped. Chalmers dropped off the rack and lost himself in the shadows. He saw Three Fingers get out and pay off the driver, then wait till the cab moved off out of sight.

Three Fingers waited a few minutes, then glided silently along the sidewalk. Chalmers stalked his man, using doorways and shadows as cover, glad of the extra screen the mist provided.

They walked in the direction of the river. The lapping of water against the jetty was an eerie murmuring in the background. Three Fingers dived into a doorway and disappeared.

When Chalmers came up to the doorway, he saw it was the side entrance to a derelict warehouse. The windows were boarded up and a half-obliterated sign swung rustily from broken hinges.

The only sound was the insidious whispering of the black waters about the wharf. The only light, a faint glimmer of yellow from the streetlamp down the block. The world was a chilled greyness — a damp shroud with death lurking everywhere.

Chalmers drew his gun and moved in on the doorway.

5

Sacrifice!

Beyond the door, a narrow passageway led into the warehouse. The floor was bare. Footprints in the dust gave him his direction. He followed the prints through an arched portal and found a flight of stone steps leading down to the cellars.

Cautiously he started down the steps. As he descended, the sound of running water became louder and he guessed he was down to river level, with only the stone wall between him and the swift-flowing Hudson.

The steps ended in another doorway. He stepped through, gun in hand, tensed for action. A heavy curtain hung across the door on the inside. He drew back the curtain and peered into the cellar.

At first, Chalmers had difficulty in making out anything at all. The room was clouded with the heavy fumes of incense burning in wall brackets. A brazier glowed redly on a dais at the far end. Strange shadows flitted through the room, weaving fantastic patterns. He heard a muttered chant rise from the dim figures standing round the dais.

Chalmers slipped past the curtain and ducked down in a dark corner, his heart thumping wildly. As his eyes became accustomed to the red light filtering through the scented smoke, he was able to identify Dr. Lanson and Three Fingers.

The doctor was standing on the dais, arms upstretched, chanting a monotonous litany. He was garbed in the exotic gown and jewelled turban he had worn the first time Chalmers had seen him. Three Fingers stood behind the doctor, and again his face was obscured by shadows. Chalmers guessed he was preparing to do his ventriloquial act.

Dr. Lanson finished his chanting. A silence fell over the congregation. Chalmers took up a position behind a stone pillar and watched as one man from the crowd went round with a tray. Each person took something from it; some a powder; some a small phial of colourless liquid; some a pipe.

The air thickened. The red glow flickered. Chalmers felt his head spin in that stifling atmosphere. He guessed what it was being handed out. *Dope!*

His eyes roved over the gathering. A dozen in all, not counting the doctor and his assistant, mostly men, but one or two women. Their faces were strained. As they indulged in the narcotic, their faces changed, became more bestial.

Chalmers felt a chill run up his spine. Was the doping the whole entertainment? Or just a preliminary? What was to follow? And where was Ann?

The sound of swift-running water sounded louder through the underground room . . .

Dr. Lanson raised his arms. In a hollow voice that echoed eerily, he began to speak:

'Tonight the Inner Circle meets for the full ritual. Once more we will indulge in the rites of the Horned One. No longer must we repress our desires to the dictates of convention.'

Chalmers eased back the safety catch on his .45. He had an idea he was going to need it shortly.

The doctor's voice ran on:

'Belchior, messenger of Darkness, are you ready to receive the obeisances of your servants?'

The curious flat voice seemed to come from the thick smoke pouring upwards from the red coals.

'Belchior hears and is ready. Belchior commands a sacrifice!'

'Death!'

The chorus surged up from eager throats. Drugged faces gleamed in the crimson glow. Chalmers shuddered. If this was what Dudley Brooks had stumbled across in his investigations, it was no wonder that he had been silenced. The flat voice ended its pronouncement:

' — Death unifies all!'

Dr. Lanson moved forward, bright eyes glittering behind the pince-nez. He left the dais and approached an alcove hidden by a black velvet cloth.

He stood in front of the alcove and raised his arms in supplication. His

50

clear-toned voice rang through the crypt.

'In the name of the Horned One, the Shadow, and the Toad that spawns in the outermost Darkness, I dedicate this sacrifice!'

The doctor whipped away the velvet cloth and a terrible chorus surged up from the congregation:

'Belchior's sacrifice!'

Chalmers came to his feet, the blood draining from his face. His lips clamped together in a thin line. His heart pounded wildly . . . the sacrifice was Ann Stevens!

Lanson brought her from the alcove. She was dressed in a long white robe and her hands were bound; her eyes were wide and mirrored the terror she felt.

Chalmers walked forward mechanically. The assembly was too intent on the girl to notice him. The gun in his hand was heavy and a strange light burned in his grey eyes.

Dr. Lanson pulled up a trapdoor in the floor and the sound of rushing water filled the chamber. They were right over the river. He pushed Ann to the edge, held her there . . .

Chalmers brought up his gun, trembling with fury.

'You will all participate,' commanded the flat voice from the curling smoke.

Lanson stepped back. The drug-takers surrounded Ann, laying hands on her. One push and she would be gone — Chalmers saw it then. Lanson could backmail these people thereafter — they had done the murder, not he!

A smile floated across the doctor's face. 'Now!' he said.

Chalmers acted instinctively. The whole scene was a blur in the red haze before him. Ann — his beloved Ann — was about to die. He fired . . .

The shot reverberated in the cellar like an avalanche roaring down a mountain slope. Dr. Lanson, a look of utter surprise on his face, reeled back and crumpled in a heap on the floor.

Pandemonium broke loose. Chalmers went on firing automatically, shooting down the dope-crazy fiends who had been about to sacrifice his love.

They shrank back before his burning eyes, leaving Ann alone. He was like a man possessed, with but one purpose in life, to reach the girl. She saw him, and hope dawned in her eyes. She moved back from the trapdoor, straining at the cords binding her.

The Satanists were too shocked by Lanson's death, too full of dope to stop him. Not so Three Fingers. The doctor's assistant, half-hidden by shadows in the background, was instantly in command of the situation. He lunged forward, bringing out a knife.

Chalmers aimed, squeezed the trigger. The hollow click of the hammer warned him the gun was empty. Hurriedly, he began to reload.

Three Fingers seized his opportunity.

'Grab him,' he yelled. 'Now's our chance — he can't hurt you — get him!'

He hurled the knife through the air. Chalmers ducked, but not fast enough. The knife grazed his temple, sending him staggering backwards. He dropped the box of shells and they scattered across the floor. Blood streamed down his face, blinding him.

He wiped his face, pushed forward,

using the empty gun as a club. White, strained faces surrounded him. Arms pulled him down. He fought them off, forced his way to the girl.

Three Fingers came at him, snarling. They clinched. Ann's eyes were on him, her lips moving in silent prayer.

Chalmers didn't try to avoid Three Fingers. Ignoring the futile grasping of the doped spectators, he sprang at Three Fingers, seized him by the throat.

Slowly, relentlessly, he forced the man's head back. Fists pummelled at his face — he hardly felt them. Suddenly Three Fingers went limp. Sweating, weak from the exertion, Chalmers let him drop to the ground.

There was a confused blur of sound. Sharp voices snapped orders. A volley of gunfire. The sound of feet running across the cellar floor.

Chalmers ignored it all. He grabbed the knife and cut the cords binding Ann. In a moment, she was in his arms, her quivering body taut against him, her lips pressed firmly on his . . .

A voice said:

'Nice work, son, you've rounded up a gang we've been after for a long time.'

Chalmers turned. The speaker was the Captain from the Homicide Bureau and the place was full of cops. He caught a glimpse of the last of the Satanists being taken away.

His face must have shown surprise for the Captain chuckled.

'If you're wondering how we turned up at just the right moment,' he said, 'it's because we've had you followed ever since you were turned loose. It was one time the old routine paid off.'

Chalmers didn't say anything. He had his arms full.

The Captain looked at Ann.

'You two lovebirds oughta get married,' he commented drily.

Ann blushed and tried to break free of his embrace.

Burt grinned and pulled her back into his arms.

'That's one swell idea,' he said, 'let's hunt up a preacher!'

He guessed from the eager pressure of her lips that the idea was all right by her.

55

2

Strange Portrait

I am writing this from a mixture of confused motives. It is not intended to be a biography of David Guest, although it will inevitably tend towards that as my story progresses. Neither is it intended as a defence of my friend against the ugly suspicions of murder that were aroused following the death of Ralph Fisher. I state here quite bluntly, that David and Ralph remained firm friends even after June Heywood decided that her choice was Ralph, for both men loved her.

Rather, I want to bring Guest's peculiar genius before a wider public, for I find very few people, even in the world of Art, have a clear idea of exactly what it was he was trying to create. And, of course, I must tell you about the strange portrait that Guest painted and the peculiar life that somehow he infused into it, and how, finally, I was driven to destroy that thing of evil.

It is difficult for me accurately to describe Guest's character, or to give a clear idea of the man himself. The difficulty is simply stated. He was a genius and I am not. I do not think that at any time during our acquaintance could I truthfully say that I apprehended one-tenth of what was going on in his head.

Perhaps it would be best if I attempt to carry the reader back in time to the moment when I was first introduced to the man. It was more than twenty years ago. I was a journalist on the staff of the *Daily News*, Ralph Fisher was Art Critic for the same paper. It was he who afforded me the introduction. Ralph and I were in the habit of meeting at the 'Blue Anchor' each Thursday night to have a few drinks and talk on mutually-interesting subjects in the warmly pleasant atmosphere of the saloon bar.

One Thursday evening, early in September, I was standing at the bar of the 'Blue Anchor' waiting for Ralph to arrive. It was past the time for our usual rendezvous, and I wondered what could be keeping him, as he was the one acquaintance of mine who was rarely late for an appointment. When he did arrive, he was in a state of great excitement, and told me the reason for his mood over a glass of ale.

'Have you ever heard of David Guest?' he asked. I shook my head: the name meant nothing to me.

'He is an artist. A creator in a new medium — no: I know what you are thinking — he does not belong to the Surrealist school, but is striving after reality in a novel manner, and I think that eventually he will succeed. He is a genius — unrecognized, as yet — because he is only in the experimental stage of his work. I want you to come along and see for yourself. Quite apart from his paintings, I know you will find him interesting: he has a fluid personality and many varied interests in life.'

Ralph was so enthusiastic over his discovery that I could not resist the temptation to go and see for myself this genius who had so completely captivated my friend — although at the time I must admit I used the term cynically.

So we went to Guest's studio.

It was a small place over an unused garage near the river. We went by taxi and climbed the wooden stairs to Guest's workshop. Ralph knocked on the door, and Guest let us in. He was not alone. An attractive brunette was with him, whom he introduced as June Heywood, an art student. She was a good-looker, and I could see that Ralph was impressed more than ordinarily. Human relations are queer things, not easily understandable, and I will make no attempt here to catch the undercurrents that were even then coming to life.

My first impression of Guest was not altogether favourable. He was lank, with hard features, dressed in a faded sports coat and flannels, with an open-necked shirt. His hair was long and unkempt, and I judged by the stubble on his face that he had not shaved since the previous day. Artistic temperament? I shrugged. His eyes were blue and held a dreamlike quality I find difficulty in expressing. And in a certain way, I suppose he was handsome.

He showed us some of his paintings. At first I did not understand them, but as I studied one after another I thought I could see his viewpoint. They were all interiors of rooms — different rooms — and though they gave me a much greater feeling of reality than I had hitherto perceived in any other picture, they all gave me the impression that there was something left out of each. I looked at them for a long time. There was complete silence. Both the girl and Ralph were obviously enthralled by Guest's work. The artist studied his audience, unsmiling.

There was a singular distortion about each painting: a distortion I could not place; it was different in each picture, yet in them all I could sense a vividness almost photographic. I tried to imagine them combined into one work. No, I do not mean that, exactly, but certain aspects of each woven into a masterpiece of creative art. Suddenly, I became aware of what it was that Guest was attempting, and I realized that if he succeeded, he would have accomplished something that no other man had ever done. I found myself agreeing with Ralph. David Guest was a genius.

That was our first meeting and it was to be by no means our last. As I look back on the past I can recall instances that impressed upon me that Guest was no ordinary man. His thoughts and ideas were not bound by convention, or pressed into a mould by the techniques of modern art. I learnt too of his many other interests, music, the sciences, particularly the sciences of biology and astronomy, literature, and of course his avid curiosity about people. But his ruling passions were painting and the Occult.

It may seem strange that he should have had such contrasting interests. Contrasting, did I say? Yet somehow, he managed to combine them to create — but I am getting ahead of myself. To enable the reader to follow this story it must be told in chronological sequence, or much of its import is missed.

He was in contact with occultists all over the world and knew intimately many investigators of unusual phenomena. I know too, he had attended meetings of strange sects who practiced ancient rites to invoke things best left undisturbed. It will be clear that his mind was not one to be rigidly confined to the more ordinary channels. That is not to imply that Guest was in any sense a crank or mystic, blinding himself to the advances of physical science. He had a firmer grasp on life than anyone else of my acquaintance, and ultimately, bent discoveries he made investigating witchcraft to his own material use.

June Heywood, the girl I first met in Guest's studio, was an enthusiastic admirer of his work, and so immersed in his art was she that she did not realize that he was rapidly falling in love with her.

My friend, Ralph Fisher, was also captivated by her charms, and the two of them went about together to shows and exhibitions, and they frequently dined together. The four of us made a queer but somehow loyal team, bonded by the genius of Guest. We met regularly, and I had the opportunity to see the intimacy ripen between Ralph and June. Although David realized what was happening it did not affect his relationship with Ralph. They remained good friends.

I can remember quite distinctly one evening when we were seated in Ralph's apartments talking. Guest as usual, led the conversation. No matter what the topic, he always took control of the talk and sent it flying into the realms of the unconventional.

'Have you ever wondered,' he said, over a glass of wine, 'whether it would be possible for an artist to imbue his painting with life? I do not mean a quality of life-likeness, for all great paintings have that — and even the best of them still remain only a painting on canvas, no matter how well executed. The difference is very subtle and I have difficulty in expressing myself. Perhaps I can put it this way. Is it possible for an artist to create within his work, a life akin to biological life? To give his pictures an animation of their own? That is very badly put, but do you see what I am driving at?'

We were seated in comfortable arm-chairs, drawn up before an open coal fire. On the table between us was a bottle of sherry and four exquisitely-cut glass tumblers. Ralph and I were smoking cigars. I leaned back in my chair trying to grasp his meaning. I think we were all rather startled, even shocked at the idea.

It was June who spoke first.

'You mean to create life? To give a portrait the ability to think and act? It sounds like the dream of some insane mystic of the Dark Ages.'

'Well, not perhaps quite that,' replied Guest. 'But you have the essential idea. I think all along I have been trying to do just that, although it's only recently I have tried to analyze the concepts I've endeavoured to portray. In my investigation of witchcraft, I came across a clue to the solution of this problem. As yet, it is too tenuous to put into words, but briefly I have found in an old manuscript certain forgotten rites, that — if I correctly construe their meaning — will enable me to put a form of life into my paintings.'

He took a sip of sherry.

'You will appreciate that every artist puts something of himself into his work, and that the pictures we call great are those where the artist has lived a full life and has managed to get more of his character and experience into his work than his contemporaries. That, however, is only a beginning. By means of this ancient secret I have unearthed, I believe that I shall be able to do more than simply put something of myself into my paintings — in short, I think I shall be able to animate them. I am seriously thinking of doing a self-portrait by this method, for I am of the impression that it will be easier for me to get life into a picture that way.'

Ralph was startled.

'That smacks of Black Magic. I mean something inherently connected with evil — isn't it likely to prove dangerous?'

That was the first time I realized that Guest's genius might lead him into paths that would prove inimical to him, and I must admit the more I thought the matter over the less I liked it. I knew that no arguments of mine would sway him from his course, so I kept silent. Often since then I have cursed myself for not making an attempt to dissuade him, even though I knew it to be useless. But God! How I wish I'd tried.

I sometimes think it would have turned out differently if Ralph and June had not told him of their intention to marry, before he started on the portrait. He congratulated them and I knew he was sincere, but it was then I think that the seed of jealousy was born deep in his subconscious. The wedding was set for three months ahead and David commenced his self-portrait. Our usual meetings broke off; Guest said he was too engrossed in his work to see anybody, and Ralph and June were too absorbed in each other to sense anything wrong. I saw him once only during that time, and then for a few minutes. He told me he was very busy and did not want to be interrupted until the picture was finished. And so we drifted apart, temporarily.

★ ★ ★

It was the week before Ralph and June were to be married that I received a telephone call from Guest. He said that the portrait was complete and enquired whether I would like to see it. Eagerly I assented and questioned him. Was it a success? He was non-committal; told me I must judge for myself, and enquired after Ralph and June, asking me to bring them along to view the new work.

The three of us went along to Guest's studio, the first time in over two months. He was alone and our greetings were warmly enthusiastic. He looked tired, as though the painting had taken something out of him. I looked about me. At the far end of the studio, facing the large bay windows stood an easel. A canvas was in position, covered by a velvet cloth. A tall adjustable mirror stood immediately to the left of the easel, and scattered over his workbench were various brushes and palettes. The room was strewn with rough sketches in varying states of preparation. I picked up one or two to study them. They were different from his previous work — there was something about them that suggested . . . I hurried to the easel where David was about to draw back the cloth.

'You must prepare for a shock,' he said in a low voice. 'I think I have been successful, and nothing like this has been done before.'

He drew back the velvet, and what lay revealed took my breath away.

It was a full-length painting of David Guest, dressed in old-fashioned style a tall, swashbuckling figure in knee breeches and blouse. A keen sword hung from a heavy leather belt, and his right hand rested on the hilt. The figure was standing in the foreground of an inn.

Painting . . . figure . . . foreground . . . Those terms are completely irrelevant. David Guest was there, alive. There was a three-dimensional effect about it; the colouring was natural, the vividness photographic. He lived!

My whole world at that moment was bounded by an inn in the Middle Ages, and there was only one other person there beside myself — David Guest. That was the effect I got, and the others got it too. We looked for long minutes drinking in that masterpiece. No one said anything. It seemed there was nothing to say. Guest had done the impossible.

We went out to dinner and thence to a local tavern where we talked of other things than art, till soon we were back on the old free and easy footing. At last the time came for 'Goodnights' and — surprise. Ralph asked David to take June home, and further asked him for the key to his studio, saying that he wanted to see the portrait again — this time alone. He pushed me off when I suggested that I should like to accompany him. So Ralph went to the studio; David took June home, and I sauntered away to my own abode pondering on the strange living picture I had seen.

★ ★ ★

At ten o'clock the following morning I received a telephone call from Guest. He asked me whether I had heard from or seen Ralph since last night. I replied in the negative, and he went on to tell me that June was at his flat looking for Ralph.

Apparently he had not been home that night and June was beginning to worry over his absence. Suggesting we go to the studio to see if he had left any indication of his whereabouts, I hired a taxi and called for David and June.

Guest went up the steps first, followed by June; I came last. The door was unlocked. David pushed it open and entered. He stopped short and June gave a stifled sob. Her face turned white. I moved forward to see what had happened.

Ralph Fisher lay on the floor in front of the painting, face upward with one leg twisted under his body. There was a long sword driven through his chest, transfixing him to the wooden floorboards. The bleeding had stopped and it was quite obvious that he had been dead several hours.

I took June in my arms to steady her. We were all shocked. I looked at Guest.

He had no eyes for his dead friend but was staring at the painting on the easel standing over Ralph's body. His gaze was riveted on the portrait and his eyes showed amazement mingled with fear. I followed his line of vision and stiffened with horror.

The figure in the picture had altered. The face was alight with an evil gloating. It was indescribably vile — as though Guest's natural jealousy of Fisher had been transferred to the portrait, and now the man David had created stood over his creator's dead enemy, glowing with triumph. The stature of the figure had altered too; it crouched with one arm uplifted to strike and — I staggered at the madness behind the thing I saw — the sword had disappeared.

I sagged limply at the impossible meaning behind that. June sat down, sobbing quietly. She took it very well considering she was to have been married in so short a while. Guest was still looking at the picture as though hypnotized by it.

'We'd better call the police,' I said, struggling back to normal. 'You take June home and look after her. I'll handle the police.'

He nodded, and taking June's arm, led her away. I hung the velvet cloth over the portrait before I dialled Whitehall. As I waited for them to arrive I wondered what they would make of it all. Of course, I did not tell them about the sword missing from the painting — I had no desire to be locked up in a madhouse! The police officials made detailed enquiries, questioning both June and myself many times. They looked for Guest but never found him. He simply vanished. Scotland Yard was very thorough they searched high and low for the missing artist but all to no avail. The mystery gradually dropped out of the headlines, and became written off as one of the unsolved murders of modern times.

As soon as it became convenient, I took that evil masterpiece to the solitude of a deserted smallholding, soaked it in petrol, and set light to it. The flames leaped upward and a pall of black smoke rose high in the sky. Was it my imagination, or did I really hear a terrible cry, like that of a lost soul, as the canvas was devoured? A gentle wind scattered the ashes wide, till no trace of Guest's portrait remained.

Unlike a piece of dramatic fiction I

cannot round this story off as I should like. I cannot say that David Guest has been cleared of the ugly rumours that associated themselves with his disappearance. Even now I do not know if he is alive, although I suspect he is still painting, buried away in some small European state. I hear tales from time to time of a great master whose work can be seen in obscure galleries, but I only ever traced one of these pictures myself.

It was in a second-hand art shop in the South of France, and I can say definitely that it was Guest's work. A painting in oils of the interior of a farmhouse with the same three-dimensional reality and in natural colouring, but without the suggestion of innate life. Even so, it had the stamp of Guest's genius that I feel sure none could copy. All my enquiries about the picture came up against a blank wall, but nevertheless I feel certain that David Guest is still alive.

What happened to June Heywood, you ask? I can see that I can no longer throw you off the trail. Yes. She is my wife.

3

The Crime At Black Dyke

Whistling the latest hit by her favourite female singer, Jo Royal swung her Alfa Romeo around the bend in the road and jammed on the brakes. The narrow country road was blocked by a crowd of women carrying banners and chanting slogans.

She stopped and stared at a demonstration in the heart of rural Shropshire.

A banner read: CHARLIE IS NOT MY DARLING!

The chanting proclaimed: 'Stop your pollution, Pearson!'

An angry woman who looked as if she had been crying glared into the car and demanded: 'Do you work for Pearson's Pesticides?'

'Not likely,' Jo said. 'I work for me. Right now I'm heading for — ' She glanced down at the map spread across her knees. ' — Black Dyke. I'm on holiday and touring, and looking for a hotel to stay the night.'

The woman thrust a leaflet through the open window. 'Then you ought to know about this.'

Jo read the flimsy sheet:

POLLUTION AT BLACK DYKE!

Charles Pearson's chemical factory is dumping poisonous waste in our town canal. Several children are in the cottage hospital, one seriously ill . . .

'Maybe I did,' Jo said, and reached for the Pentax camera on the seat beside her. 'I'm a freelance journalist when I'm working.'

'That's great — maybe you can get us some publicity. I'm Ann Shephard. I'll guide you into Black Dyke.'

She handed her bundle of leaflets to one of the other women, opened the car door and got in.

'Clear the road, Maureen. I'm taking a journalist to the hospital.'

After the women moved aside, Jo drove forward, past the wrought-iron gates of a large country house.

'That's where Pearson lives when he's home,' Ann said. 'Charles Pearson — you must have heard of him.'

'Vaguely,' Jo said. 'Refresh my memory.'

'He reckons he's the Lord of the Manor in this part of the country. His great-grandfather started a small chemical factory. When Charlie took control, he went to the City and came back with money to expand and develop. His factory has done well, selling fertilizers and pesticides all round the world, and he's after a knighthood. He's rich enough to buy people off.'

'No one buys me off,' Jo said. 'Feed me some facts.'

The car passed over a humpbacked bridge crossing a narrow canal. The water was scummy and an unpleasant smell arose from it. Adults patrolled the towpath, chasing children away.

'When I was a kid, we always played along the canal bank,' Ann said. 'Now, it's too dangerous.'

The road entered a street lined by terraced houses and shops. Black Dyke was a market town, dominated by the tanks and pipes of an immense chemical plant. Jo noted the *Talbot*, a four-star hotel.

The cottage hospital was at the far end of the town, a small modern building. Jo parked in the drive and Ann Shepherd got out, moving at a brisk trot. Jo followed.

A woman was talking to a man in a white coat at reception.

'How is she, Sarah?' Ann asked.

'As well as can be expected,' the doctor said quickly.

'What does that mean?'

'She's still seriously ill. I can't allow visitors.'

Ann turned to Jo. 'This doctor's been bought. Because Pearson paid for this hospital, he thinks it doesn't matter how many of our kids are poisoned.'

The doctor looked uneasy. 'That's not fair. The town needs this hospital, and without Mr. Pearson — '

'Tough,' Jo said. 'But life never was simple. Let me see your patient, and maybe I can do something to help.'

Jo opened her handbag and selected a card which read:

JO ROYAL
Photo-journalist

The doctor hesitated briefly, then said: 'Very well. We've nothing to hide — you can see her, but that's all. And please leave my name out of this.'

'Of course, doctor.'

He led the way down a passage and opened a door. It was a small private ward, with a nurse in attendance. A girl of about seven lay in bed, her face pale and her eyes wide open.

'Mummy,' she said. 'I'm hurting . . . '

Sarah began to cry, and the doctor gestured them to leave and closed the door.

Ann said angrily, 'Are you doing anything for her?'

'Everything we can.' The doctor looked unhappy. 'Some of those industrial chemicals are very complex compounds.'

Outside, Jo said, 'Something ought to be done about Charles Pearson.'

Ann shrugged. 'He's clever. He makes a big thing about avoiding polluting the countryside — and people believe him.'

Jo smiled. 'Tell me about him. Every man has his weakness . . . '

* * *

Jo booked in at the *Talbot* and got Pearson's personal assistant on the phone. It took only a mention of a rumour about a knighthood to Pearson. Another mention of a national magazine and she was granted an interview.

After a breakfast of champagne and pomegranate, Jo drove off to Pearson's country house with her camera and a shorthand notebook.

She approached the house slowly, studying the cover. Behind stone walls were a lot of trees and bushes. The windows were high and narrow, with ivy covering the walls. There'd be no trouble getting into the house.

She parked and went up the steps between fluted columns. A uniformed security man with a truncheon at his belt opened the door.

Pearson waited for her in the lounge, beside a drinks cabinet. Jo, wearing a business suit, assumed an appearance of cool professionalism.

Charles Pearson looked like an elderly

cherub with snow-white hair, but cold grey eyes revealed another side to his character.

She accepted a sherry and sipped slowly, gazing around the room, aware of a musty smell.

'So, Ms. Royal, what sort of a story are you looking for?'

'A personal story. Your family and background.' Jo spoke earnestly. 'Your ancestors. How the business started — how you developed it.'

Pearson swallowed his sherry in one gulp and stood up.

'Yes, I'm proud of my ancestors, proud of the family home.' He indicated the room and its antique furniture with a sweep of his arm. 'The Pearsons go back a long way. Right now, my personal assistant is engaged in drawing up a family tree for — you know what. It was my great-grandfather who started it, in a small way of business, of course. That's his portrait over the mantelpiece.'

Jo stared at a framed oil painting from which a face peered out through a layer of discoloured varnish. It might have been a portrait of Scrooge, she thought; a pointed nose, shrivelled cheeks and thin lips.

'Simon Pearson, painted by Sir Thomas Lawrence. The experts tell me it's worth money. But what's money? I wouldn't part with that painting for a million pounds. When I look at old Simon, I see myself.'

Jo had trained herself to estimate measurements accurately, and she jotted down figures in her notebook.

She raised her camera.

'Will you pose for me? Beside the painting.'

'With pleasure,' he said, proudly,

She took several shots, including one of the painting on its own.

'Our female readers would be thrilled to learn something about your house . . . '

Pearson gave her a conducted tour, and Jo's camera snapped the detail she needed. The passages were on different levels; doors led off to additions to the original building. There was no alarm system, and no dogs; apparently he relied for security on his thugs armed with truncheons.

He showed her the wine cellar, padlocked. A child could have opened it with a hairpin. At the rear of the cellar she saw a number of old paintings covered in dust.

As she was about to leave, Jo said, 'The women of Black Dyke accuse you of poisoning the canal. Some of the town children are in hospital. Would you like to comment?'

Pearson's face coloured with anger. His words cane out like an explosion.

'Absolute rubbish! My factory provides work for the men of Black Dyke. Their hospital was built with my money. Of course I don't pollute their stinking canal. These women are freaks, do-gooders, libbers — stupid! I'll never give in to them. Never!'

Jo Royal smiled.

*　*　*

From Black Dyke, she drove back to London and got her film developed. She asked for a large blow-up of old Simon's portrait and took it to a painting friend in

Chelsea, who specialized in copying Old Masters.

'Could be Lawrence,' Billy Baines said. 'Or it might be a copy after him. I'd have to see the original to be sure.'

Jo flipped open her notebook and gave him the measurements. 'Can you paint me a copy? Exactly as is, brown varnish and all?'

'No problem. I'll do it for you over the weekend. Okay?'

'Okay.'

★ ★ ★

Jo relaxed aboard her motor cruiser moored on the Thames. On Monday morning she visited Billy Baines again and admired his handiwork.

'It won't pass scrutiny by an expert,' he warned.

'If everything goes according to plan, it won't have to,' she said. 'Now, I want to borrow some tools to remove a canvas and replace it with this.'

'I'll want them back.'

'Of course, Billy.'

88

Back aboard her cruiser, Jo studied Billy's copy again. Simon Pearson sneered at her from beneath thick brown varnish.

'You're about to become famous, Scrooge,' she murmured.

She used the radio-phone to make an overnight booking at the *Talbot*. Then she rang Ann Shephard and invited her to dinner at the hotel.

Her Alfa Romeo covered the miles to Shropshire at a comfortable seventy for most of the motorway. She booked in and relaxed in a hot bath, then dressed for dinner.

Over gammon steak, fresh fruit with cream and coffee, Jo said, 'I can do something about Charlie Pearson — but I'm going to need your help.'

'Anything,' Ann said fervently.

'I'm not going into detail. The less you know the better if the police should ask questions afterwards. What I want is a diversion.'

Ann's eyes opened wide as she listened.

'That's easy enough. I'm good at organising demos . . . '

★　★　★

Jo was up early next morning. She dressed in tracksuit and trainers, checked she had Billy's tools and the rolled up canvas in her holdall and jogged out of town.

At dawn, she scaled the wall surrounding the grounds of Pearson's house. She moved quickly and silently to a tree growing close to the house and shinned up it. She straddled a branch among dense foliage and settled to wait.

Presently she heard chanting, and saw a crowd of women marching along the road. She watched as Ann used a tyre lever to force open the wrought-iron gates. The demonstrators swarmed into the grounds and spread out, carrying banners and chanting a new slogan:

'Poisonous Pearson is a pest!'

A couple of security men ran out of the lodge and the women scattered among the trees and bushes. A cameraman from a photographic agency was with them, shooting pictures. More security men came from the house, truncheons drawn.

Jo slid down the trunk of her tree and darted into the house. She went directly to the empty lounge, and lifted down old Simon's portrait and carried it to the door. The house was quiet.

She moved along the passage to the steps leading down to the cellar. Her picklock opened the door in seconds and she switched on the light and closed the door after her.

She moved to the rear of the cellar and started work. Taking the old canvas out of its frame, she used pliers to remove the tacks holding the canvas to its stretcher. Then, working quickly, she placed Billy's copy over the stretcher and nailed it in place using steel tacks and a hammer. She used corner wedges to tighten the canvas and slid it back into the heavy frame. She used spit to smear dust over the shiny new nails, then hid the portrait among the other paintings stacked at the back of the cellar.

She put Billy's tools into her holdall along with the rolled-up canvas and took a final look round. There was no sign she had been there. She switched off the light and eased open the door. She heard distant shouting. She relocked the cellar and left the house.

In the grounds she saw a security man hitting a woman with his truncheon. Two other demonstrators pulled him away. The photographer's camera snapped them.

'Get that camera!' another security man shouted.

Jo signalled to Ann, who called, 'Everybody leave!'

Ann and Jo ran interference for the cameraman.

'Move,' Jo hissed. 'Get that photo to the London papers.'

She joined the exodus.

*   *   *

Aboard her motor cruiser at Chelsea, Jo unrolled the stolen canvas. In places the paint had cracked; a job for Michael Cade, she decided.

She smiled as she looked at the daily papers. The picture of Pearson's security man hitting a woman was on the front page, and Pearson was quoted:

'The guard was over-excited. You must

remember that these women were on private property. Of course my factory has never polluted the canal ... the demonstrators stole a valuable painting and I shan't rest until I have recovered it.'

Jo typed an open letter to Pearson:

Your painting will be returned immediately you acknowledge responsibility for the polluted canal at Black Dyke.

She sent copies to all the daily papers and national television studios. It got maximum publicity and a quick answer from Pearson:

'I agree. I am taking steps to avoid further pollution — and will personally see that the canal is cleaned out.'

His cherubic face came over well on the screen. He might still get his knighthood, Jo thought. While waiting for Ann to report that the canal was clean again, she took the original to Michael at Cade's auction house.

He inspected the cracks in the surface and said, 'There's another painting beneath this, Jo. I doubt if this is a genuine Lawrence, so I'll take a chance and see what's underneath.'

Jo heard from Ann and wrote to Pearson, telling him to look in his wine cellar. She had no fear of repercussions; the painting of old Simon was in its original frame and had never left the house. There would be no need to have it examined by an expert.

Later, Michael phoned. 'I've got something to show you.'

She called at the auction rooms where a painting rested on an easel. Gone was old Scrooge.

She saw an oil sketch of a buxom female nude, painted in glowing pinks.

'A real find,' Michael said. 'A Rubens sketch for one of his paintings. It'll bring a good price at auction. You know, the real crime at Black Dyke was to cover a Rubens nude with that awful face . . . '

'Typical,' Jo said. 'Just like a man.'

4

Time For Murder

The corpse was dressed in a well-cut suit of black pinstripe, with white shirt, stiff collar and black bow tie. It lay across a Persian rug with the pointed toes of patent leather shoes aimed at the ceiling. A neat round hole, rust-brown at the edges, spoilt the freshly laundered shirt.

Inspector Burton listened attentively while the local constable read aloud from his notebook.

'Gerald Laver, age sixty-three, financier, bachelor, lived alone except for one servant. Shot through the heart from a distance of three yards by a .45 automatic — that's the gun on the table — died instantly. Time of death established by medical evidence, nine to nine-thirty p.m. Wrist watch smashed and stopped at nine-twenty-one p.m.'

Burton glanced at his own watch. It was ten-thirty-two. 'An hour ago. How did you get here so fast?'

'Tip-off by 'phone — anonymous, of course.'

'The servant?'

'No. He was at the cinema — arrived back at ten-oh-three. We were here before that.'

Burton's gaze shifted from the two C.I.D. men taking measurements to the gun lying on the table top.

'Any prints?'

'Yes, good and clear — he'll swing for this.'

'Motive?'

'Established — this case is so easy, a recruit out of Hendon could wrap it up! Papers in the desk show that Clifford Webb, a research physicist, was heavily in debt to Laver, that tonight repayment fell due. With Laver dead, he doesn't have to pay a penny.'

'Sounds too easy. Where's the catch?'

The constable shook his head. 'No catch.'

'All right,' Burton said. 'Let's pick up Webb.'

*   *   *

They picked up Webb. The prints on the gun were his. The serial number proved he had bought the gun only a week before. He admitted that he was in debt to Laver.

Cliiford Webb was arrested, charged with the murder of Gerald Laver and brought to trial.

He pleaded not guilty and, when the question of timing was brought out, caused a sensation by proving conclusively that he was nowhere near Laver's house at nine-twenty-one on the night of the murder.

As a member of the Royal Society, he had arrived at Burlington House at ten minutes to eight, listened with a hundred other members to Professor Smythe's paper — then, at eight-forty-five, commenced reading his own paper on *Thermodynamics for a Space-Time Continuum*. He finished reading the paper at nine thirty-five, answered a number of questions and left Burlington House shortly after ten o'clock. With more than a hundred witnesses, his alibi could not be broken.

Clifford Webb was acquitted of a charge of murder.

* * *

Inspector Burton stared glumly at his desk and wondered how the gun that had killed Laver could clearly show Webb's fingerprints, and no others, if Webb had not been the last man to handle it. He already had a headache from thinking about that.

His sergeant brought him a mug of sweetened tea. 'Tough time with the commissioner, inspector?'

'The old man damn near read me the book. It's a perishing wonder I'm not pounding a beat again!'

The sergeant clucked like a sympathetic hen. 'Odd sort of case, inspector. If it weren't for that alibi — '

Burton spluttered and slammed down his mug of tea. It slopped over the desk, ruining a report he was working on. 'Don't mention alibis to me!'

The sergeant offered his cigarettes. Burton took one, flicked the wheel of his lighter and inhaled gratefully. The sergeant waited a few seconds, then said, hesitantly: 'There was another odd thing I noticed — '

He paused.

'Yes?' prompted the inspector.

'I didn't mention it before because it seemed crazy — it still does, but maybe you ought to know about it. After you'd left Laver's house, I was alone with the corpse, waiting for the mortuary van to come. It was quiet in that room. Just me and the deceased — then, all at once, there was this rabbit.'

'Rabbit! What rabbit?' Burton stared at the sergeant. 'Did you say, rabbit?' he repeated.

'That's right, sir — a fluffy white rabbit with pink eyes and long ears. It was running round the room, then, suddenly — it wasn't there any more. Vanished right under my nose!'

Burton looked at his sergeant long and hard. 'Drinking intoxicating liquor on duty?' he suggested.

'No, sir, hadn't touched a drop.'

Burton thought of the fingerprints on

Webb's automatic . . . and now a white rabbit!

'You're not suggesting it was the rabbit who shot Gerald Laver?'

'Of course not, sir. But it does seem odd, that rabbit coming from nowhere and then disappearing. I just thought I'd mention it.'

Burton stubbed out his cigarette, taking his time about it, but before he could think of an adequate reply, the telephone rang. He picked up the receiver. 'Yes . . . speaking. Who? I see . . . I'll come over right away. Goodbye.'

He cradled the 'phone thoughtfully, turning to the sergeant. 'Guess who?' he invited.

'The commissioner?'

Burton glared. 'You've a lousy sense of humour. No, that was Clifford Webb, and he wants me to call on him.'

'Perhaps he wants to confess?' the sergeant suggested.

*   *   *

Clifford Webb was a head taller than Burton, a rangy man with a sharply-pointed nose

102

and eyes that never quite seemed to focus in one place. He was wearing a white laboratory coat as he greeted the inspector.

'Nice of you to spare the time, inspector. Can I offer you a drink?'

'Thanks, no.'

Webb grinned sardonically.

'Could be you object to drinking with a murderer!'

Burton refused to be drawn. Looking round the comfortably furnished room, he asked: 'What did you want to see me about?'

Webb waved him to a chair, then moved across to the fireplace. His eyes focused briefly on Burton's face.

'As I understand the law,' he said, 'now that I have been acquitted of Laver's murder, I cannot again be charged with that crime. Correct?'

Burton nodded.

'Good! Now, inspector, prepare yourself for a shock. I did kill Gerald Laver — and I'll tell you how.'

Burton took a cigarette from his case and lit it. 'Just why are you telling me this?' he asked, bluntly.

'Vanity, inspector, pure vanity. I have committed the perfect crime. Naturally I want you to know — now that you can't do a damn thing about it! I thought you might have guessed from the title of the paper I read to the Royal Society. Remember? It was called *Thermodynamics for a Space-Time Continuum*. Time, inspector, that's the clue you missed . . .

'Time is an imperfectly understood medium. Perhaps dimension would be a better word. The fourth dimension, it is usually called. An object can have its position in space fixed by the dimensions of length, breadth and depth — but unless we say that it exists in this space for a certain *time*, how can we say that its position is fixed at all?'

Burton declined to answer.

'I have long desired to experiment with the dimension of time, to travel through the fourth dimension as we now travel through space, and it was Laver who gave me the opportunity. He advanced the money for my experiments. He wanted a machine that would travel into the past, thinking by this means to cheat death and attain immortality! He did not realise that such a transference would automatically set up a new future for himself, involving a new death.

'For myself, I was interested in the practical applications for crime. Not that I have any interest in crime, as such, but scientific research costs money and I saw the chance of getting that money. For instance, I could commit a robbery in the present, then retreat into the past and fix an unbreakable alibi. Interested, inspector?'

Burton nodded, shredding the end of his cigarette with his teeth.

'I succeeded,' Clifford Webb continued. 'I built my machine, and now, if you will follow us, I'll show it to you. But don't expect anything spectacular — this isn't Hollywood.'

Burton followed the physicist through a door and along a passage to the laboratory. In the centre of the room, he saw a doorframe surrounded by the coils of wire helices. A control panel was marked off in an elaborate time-scale.

'Doesn't look much, does it, inspector?

But I can assure you it works.'

Burton looked at Webb and knew that if he wasn't dealing with a madman then he was with a murderer.

'How?' he grunted.

'The maths involved are of a very high order,' Webb said, 'so you must be content with analogies. When I pass an electric current through my helices, a field of energy is created which distorts the space-time continuum. Space as well as time, you will note. In effect, I can step through my door frame into another time and arrive at a different location from this room!'

'I still don't see how you faked your alibi,' Burton grunted.

'But it's so simple, inspector. I had already decided to kill Laver — he was threatening to foreclose on his loan. I attended the Royal Society, arriving back here about half-past ten. I adjusted the time-scale of my machine to nine-twenty, the space location to Laver's study. Then I stepped through.'

Webb's eyes glittered, his breath quickened.

'As I expected, I was in Gerald Laver's study — and he was taken completely by surprise. I shot him, 'phoned the police and returned here. I had only to wait for you to prove my alibi!'

'I still don't see how you could be in two places at once,' Burton said.

'How can I explain it? Time is not like a river flowing in one direction. Think of it as a tapestry; the flow of time corresponds to the warp, the lengthwise threads — but there is also the woof, the crosswise threads. These represent our position in the time-stream — and note please that the warp has *infinite* threads. Perhaps you can imagine it as a series of parallel worlds; we have a possible existence in each but are only aware of one! I killed Laver in another world, on a different warp of the tapestry . . . things might have gone wrong, I admit. When I returned, Laver might not have died in this world. My interference with time could have upset my alibi. Perhaps I would have been stranded in that space-time where I killed Laver. Anything might have happened, but I was lucky and it worked out the way I planned.'

Burton threw away the butt of his cigarette. 'And now that you've been acquitted, you are perfectly safe,' he said, slowly. 'Yes, you're right — it is a perfect crime.'

Webb smiled complacently.

'Perhaps you'd like to see a demonstration, inspector?'

Burton nodded, and the physicist switched on the power and made an adjustment to the time-scale. The helices began to glow and, between the limits of the doorframe, appeared a blackness so intense that the Inspector could not bear to look into it.

Webb removed a white rabbit from a hutch on his work bench.

'Daisy,' he said, smoothing back the rabbit's long ears, 'is the world's most experienced time-traveller. I've used her for many experiments and she has always returned unharmed. I doubt if she knows what a remarkable rabbit she is!'

Burton stared, remembering his sergeant's story. The hairs at the nape of his neck began to bristle.

'I am sending her back to a period a little after the time of the murder,' Webb said, 'the location as before . . . Laver's study. Perhaps one of your men reported seeing Daisy? In which case, we mustn't disappoint him . . . ' He set Daisy on the floor before the door into time and gently urged her through it. Instantly, she vanished from view.

Burton walked warily round the door in the centre of the room. He completed a full circuit without seeing anything of Daisy.

'Convinced, inspector? She will appear again in one minute — I have set the automatic control for that period.'

The seconds ticked by. Burton studied the time-scale carefully; a plan was shaping in his head, a plan to bring Clifford Webb to justice.

'Here she is, inspector!' the physicist exclaimed triumphantly.

He lifted the rabbit from the floor and placed her back inside her hutch.

Burton moved silently and, as Webb turned from the hutch, swung his fist to the physicist's jaw. Webb slumped unconscious to the floor.

Burton studied the controlling mechanism of the time machine yet again. It seemed simple enough. He adjusted the time-scale for nine-twenty of the night of the murder. Webb had already told him that the space location was Laver's study. He had only to step through to catch the murderer red-handed.

He took one last look at the unconscious form of Clifford Webb and stepped between the glowing helices into blackness . . .

There was the Persian rug, but Laver was not now stretched out upon it. The financier faced Clifford Webb, staring fascinated at the gun in his hand. Webb's finger tightened on the trigger.

'Stop!'

The command was torn from Burton's lips as if of its own volition. Webb half-turned, amazement written plain across his face — and, in that moment of hesitation, Laver hurled himself across the room to grapple with his would-be murderer.

Burton heard the shot, and saw one of the two men stagger and fall across the

Persian rug. He looked down.

The corpse had been a rangy man with a sharply pointed nose. The eyes, which in life had never quite seemed to focus in one place, were now focused in death on the ceiling. Clifford Webb had paid in full for his intended crime.

'It was self-defence!' Gerald Laver screamed. 'You saw it — he threatened me — I killed him in self-defence!'

Inspector Burton scratched his head and wondered what the commissioner would make of his report.

5

The Circus

Because he had been drinking, Arnold Bragg considered it a stroke of good fortune that the accident happened a long way from any main road and the chance of a patrolling police car. He had no exact idea of his location, just that it was somewhere in the West Country.

He was on his way back from Cornwall where he'd been covering a story, an exposé of a witches' coven, for the *Sunday Herald*. He drove an MG sports car and, as always with a few drinks inside him, drove too fast. With time to spare, he'd left the A30 at a whim. It was a summer evening, slowly cooling after the heat of the day. The countryside was what he called 'pretty', with lanes twisting between hedgerows. He took a corner at speed and rammed the trunk of a tree that jutted into the road around the bend.

Shaken but unhurt, he climbed from his car and swore at a leaking radiator.

Then he got back in and drove on, looking for a garage. He found one, a couple of miles further along, next to a pub with a scattering of cottages; there were not enough of them to justify calling them a village.

A mechanic glanced at the bonnet and sniffed his breath. 'Ar, I can fix it. Couple of hours, maybe.'

Arnold Bragg nodded. 'I'll be next door when you've finished.'

It was the kind of pub that exists only in out-of-the-way places, and then rarely: a house of local stone with a front room converted as a bar. The door stood open and he walked in past a stack of beer crates. The walls were thick and it was cool inside. On a polished counter rested two casks, one of cider and one of beer. A grey-haired woman sat knitting behind the counter, and two oldish men sat on a wooden bench by the window.

Bragg turned on a charm that rarely failed him. 'I'll try a pint of your local beer.'

The woman laid her knitting aside, picked up a glass mug and held it under the tap; sediment hung in the rich brown liquid.

Bragg tasted it, then drank deeply. 'I didn't know anyone still brewed beer like this.' He glanced around the room.

'Perhaps you gentlemen will join me?'

'Ar, likely we will, sir. And many thanks.'

Bragg's gaze moved on to a poster thumb-tacked to the wall. It had obviously been hand-printed, and read:

CIRCUS
Before your very eyes,
werewolf into man!
See the vampire rise from his coffin!
Bring the children —
invest in a sense of wonder

As Arnold Bragg stared and wondered if beer had finally rotted his brain, sluggish memory stirred. In his job, he always listened to rumours; some he hunted down and obtained a story. There had been this crazy one, crazy but persistent, of a freak circus that never visited towns but stopped only for one night at isolated villages. He'd come across it first in the Fens, then on the

Yorkshire moors, and again in a Welsh valley.

The knowledge that this circus was here, now, sobered him. He set down his glass on the counter, unfinished. When he scented a lead, he could stop drinking. And this one was likely to prove the apex of a career dedicated to discrediting fakes and phonies of all kinds.

He studied the poster carefully. No name was given to the circus. There was no indication of time or place of performance. Still, it shouldn't be hard to find.

He strolled outside, passed the garage where the mechanic worked on his car, and sauntered towards the cottages. A few families, young husbands and wives with their offspring, were walking down a lane, and he followed them. Presently he glimpsed, in the distance, the canvas top of a large tent showing above some trees.

He kept to himself, observing the people on the way to the circus; there was no gaiety in them. With solemn faces and measured step they went, people who took their pleasure seriously.

Beyond a screen of trees was a green

field with the big top and a huddle of caravans and Land Rovers. People formed a small queue at an open flap of the tent, where a little old man sold tickets. He sported a fringe of white hair, nut-brown skin and the wizened appearance of a chimpanzee.

Bragg dipped a hand into his pocket and brought out some loose change.

'I don't believe you'll like our show, sir.' The accent was foreign. 'It's purely for the locals, you understand. Nothing sophisticated for a London gentleman.'

'You're wrong,' Bragg said, urging money on him. 'This is just right for me.' He snatched a ticket and walked into the tent.

Seats rose in tiers, wooden planks set on angle-irons. In the centre was a sawdust ring behind low planking; an aisle at the rear allowed performers to come and go. There was no provision for a high-wire act.

Bragg found an empty seat away from the local people, high enough so that he commanded a clear view, but not so far from the ringside that he would miss any detail.

Not many seats were occupied. He lit a cigarette and watched the crowd. Grave faces, little talk; the children showed none of that excitement normally associated with a visit to the circus. Occasionally eyes turned his way and were hastily averted. A few more families arrived, all with young children.

The old man who sold tickets doubled as ringmaster. He shuffled across the sawdust and made his announcement in hardly more than a whisper. Bragg had to strain to catch the words.

'I, Doctor Nis, welcome you to my circus. Tonight you will see true wonders. The natural world is full of prodigies for those who open their eyes and minds. We begin with the vampire.'

Somewhere, pipe music played; notes rippled up and down a non-Western scale, effecting an eerie chant. Two labourers came down the aisle, carrying a coffin. The coffin was far from new and they placed it on the ground as if afraid it might fall to pieces.

The pipes shrilled.

Bragg found he was holding his breath

and forced himself to relax. Tension came again as the lid of the coffin moved. It moved upwards, jerkily, an inch at a time. A thin hand with long fingernails appeared from inside. The lid was pushed higher, creaking in the silence of the tent, and the vampire rose and stepped out.

Its face had the pallor of death, the canine teeth showed long and pointed, and a ragged cloak swirled about its human form.

One of the labourers returned with a young lamb and tossed it to the vampire. Hungrily, teeth sank into the lamb's throat, bit deep, and the lips sucked and sucked . . .

Bragg stared, fascinated and disgusted. When, finally, the drained carcase was tossed aside, the vampire appeared swollen as a well-filled leech.

The labourers carried the coffin out and the vampire walked behind. Jesus, Bragg thought — this is for kids?

Dr. Nis made a small bow.

'You who are present tonight are especially fortunate. Not at every performance is it possible to show a shape-changer. Lycanthropy is not a condition that can be perfectly timed — and now, here is the werewolf.'

He placed a small whistle to his lips and blew into it. No sound came, but a large grey wolf trotted into the sawdust ring, moving as silently as the whistle that called it. Slanting eyes glinted yellowish-green. The animal threw back its head and gave a prolonged and chilling howl.

Hairs prickled on the back of Bragg's neck and he almost came out of his seat. He blinked his eyes as the wolf-shape wavered. The creature appeared to elongate as it rose high on its hind limbs. The fur changed. Bragg moistened suddenly-dry lips as the wolf became more manlike . . . and more . . . till it was a naked man who stood before them.

An attendant draped a blanket about his shoulders and together they walked off. Blood pounded through Bragg's head; it had to be a fake, obviously, but it was a convincing fake.

'The ancient Egyptians believed in physical immortality,' Dr. Nis whispered. 'They had a ceremony known as the Opening of the Mouth. This ceremony restored to the body, after death, its ability to see, hear, eat and speak. Here now, a mummy from the land of the Pharaohs.'

A withered mummy, wrapped in discoloured linen bandages, its naked face dark-skinned, was carried into the ring. Four jars were placed about it.

'These are canopic jars, containing the heart and lungs and the viscera of the deceased.'

A voice spoke, a voice that seemed to come from the mummy. It spoke in a language unfamiliar to Bragg.

Dr. Nis said smoothly: 'I will translate freely. The mummy speaks: True believers only are safe here — those who doubt are advised to open their hearts.'

Bragg wanted to laugh, but sweat dried cold on his flesh and laughter wouldn't come.

The mummy was carried off.

'We have next,' Dr. Nis said with pride, 'an experiment of my own. Can a corpse be re-animated? Can the component parts of a man be brought together and endued with life? I shall allow you to judge how successful I have been.'

A travesty of a man shuffled down the aisle and into the ring. It was hideous. The limbs were not identical; they had not come from the same body. The head, waxen and discoloured, lolled at an angle, as if insecurely hinged at the neck. It lumbered unsteadily around the sawdust ring, and it smelt. The man-thing did not speak; it stumbled over uneven feet, rocking from side to side as it tried to recover balance, and lost its head.

A small gasp was jerked from Bragg's lips as the detached head hit the sawdust and rolled to a stop. The headless cadaver blundered on aimlessly, like a decapitated chicken, until attendants hurried to guide it from the ring.

Bragg felt sick, and his fingers drummed nervously on his knees. Impossible to believe the thing was just a freak; yet he had to believe, or admit the impossible.

Dr. Nis looked unhappy. 'I must apologize — obviously my experiment is not yet perfected for public viewing. And so we come to our final offering this evening. You all know, if only in a vague way, that before men inhabited this world, the reptiles ruled for millions of years. They were the true Lords of the Earth. Science maintains that they died out before men appeared, but science has been wrong before. There was interbreeding . . . '

The creature that slithered into the ring was about five feet long. It had the general appearance of a man on all fours, but its skin was scaly and iridescent. The hands were clawed, the head narrowed and thrust forward, and a forked tongue hung from the mouth.

An attendant brought a plastic bag and released from it a cloud of flies. The creature reared up, long tongue flickering like forked lightning, catching the flies and swallowing them.

A sick show, Bragg decided; an outrage to perform this sort of thing before children. The catchphrases of popular journalism ran through his head — **This Show Must Be Banned!**

Pipe music played again, a falling scale. Dr. Nis bowed and left the ring. Families rose and filed quietly out, their offspring subdued.

Bragg vaulted into the ring, crossed the sawdust and left by the aisle exit. As he hurried towards the caravans, he saw Dr. Nis entering one of them.

The door was just closing when Bragg arrived and leaned on it. Dr. Nis turned to peer at him.

'Ah, Mr. Bragg, I was half-expecting you. You are, after all, well known in your trade.'

Bragg pushed his way into the caravan and felt like a giant in a doll's house; everything seemed smaller, neat and tidy in its appointed place.

'Then you'll know the paper I work for and the sort of thing I write.' He couldn't be bothered to turn on the charm. 'Tell me — tell the *Herald*'s millions of readers — how do you justify your show? Horror for adults — OK, we'll go along with that. But the kids?'

Dr. Nis made a small deprecating motion with his hands. 'Horror, Mr. Bragg? I deplore the term. My life is spent trying to keep alive a faith, a faith in the mystery of Nature. Strange things happen. If a man who believes sees a

126

ghost, is he frightened? Yet a man who disbelieves and comes face to face with one may well die of shock. So perhaps my show serves a useful purpose . . . as for children, what better time to develop a sense of wonder?'

'That's your story — now let's have the low-down on how your gimmicks work.'

'Gimmicks?' Dr. Nis regarded him calmly. 'I assure you I do not deal in trickery. Consider this: who knows you are here? And aren't you just a little bit frightened?'

Bragg flinched. 'Who, me? Of a bunch of freaks?' But his voice was edged with doubt.

Dr. Nis said, 'I do not want the kind of publicity you have in mind, Mr. Bragg. I don't think it would serve my purpose.' He smiled suddenly, and his smile was not for his visitor.

Arnold Bragg turned. Freaks crowded the door of the caravan: the vampire, the werewolf and the lizard-man. The resurrected man was conspicuously absent.

'I think it would be best if Mr. Bragg disappeared,' Dr. Nis said quietly. 'But don't damage his head, please.' He looked again at Bragg, his eyes bright and hard.

'You see, Mr. Bragg, I believe I have a use for it.'

6

The Active Man

He glowed. Geigers rattled as he passed. He was the Active Man.

A gunshot boomed and dust spurted at his feet as the bullet ricocheted. Close, he thought, too close; and broke cover and ran between the concrete walls of Admin and No. 1 laboratory. A second bullet followed him into the temporary cover afforded by a parked wagon.

That would be Garside, he thought dully. Garside was desperate; trust Garside to have a gun and know how to use it.

The bullets came near but none touched him. It was almost as if those tiny buttons of lead knew it was no use trying for a dead man. Six hours the doctor had said. *Six hours left to live.* He tried counting how much longer he had but time no longer registered with him.

There was a burning pain in his flesh and his limbs obeyed sluggishly. He was a dead man living on borrowed time and he had a job to do before the end came. He moved again, taking up a fresh position, working his way nearer those two lead-lined suitcases.

Shadowy forms closed in; laboratory workers in protective clothing with shiny metal claws for handling the 'hot' stuff. They were after him! Hunted like an animal . . . no, not like an animal . . . like a piece of waste matter that had somehow slipped out of the radioactive labs.

He laughed wildly as he ran free. A voice boomed over the loudspeakers:

'Give yourself up, Martin. We appeal to you not to endanger the lives of other men.'

The whiplash of Garside's automatic sounded again. Garside didn't want him taken alive.

He was near the main gate now. He could see the two suitcases and a small, thin man with sharp features — the agent provocateur. He was in time; he had to be in time. His legs were unsteady, burning. *Disintegration of the body cells*, the doctor had called it. He was falling apart.

Oh God, he thought, *Ruth*!
Now —
He hurled himself at the agent provocateur.

★ ★ ★

Frank Martin was a callow youth with the pimples of adolescence not yet clear of his face. He had no idea what he wanted of life beyond marrying his girl and setting up home. He worked as a cleaner at the atomic weapons establishment known as Garside Enterprises and didn't much care for the job, but stuck it because the pay was good.

Ruth, of course, didn't know he was a cleaner. He hadn't actually lied, but the few casual hints he had supplied — hints only, because the establishment had secrecy rules — suggested that he was engaged upon important research work.

Three evenings each week and all day Sunday he spent with Ruth in the village where she lived, five miles away. She was young and pretty with curling brown hair and he had asked her to marry him the second time they met. Sometimes she would talk about his work and ask him how it felt to make atom bombs.

Martin replied vaguely that he supposed it was all right; that we had to protect ourselves from the newly-formed alliance of the eastern hemisphere. But he never really thought about the implications of his job.

The establishment was isolated, in a valley between high mountains. In Spring, melting snow slid down the slopes and set the rivers racing in a mad torrent; in Winter, the peaks were all tinsel-silver and blue shadow. It was a lovely part of the country.

Garside Enterprises was a private concern; to be sure, there were government inspectors and a security patrol, but the firm operated privately and the profits went into the pockets of Henry Garside. Frank Martin cleaned out the laboratories in a suit designed to protect him from stray radiation, collected his pay check and planned to marry his girl. Life was very simple if you didn't think about consequences.

One evening, cleaning up after the

chemists had left, Frank Martin knocked over an expensive piece of equipment. He didn't know what it was called, but there were coils of glass tubing and filters and a measuring gauge. He was horrified, visualizing the loss of pay he would suffer if his accident were discovered.

In a state of panic, he set about sweeping up the debris. The waste bin was outside, back of the building, and it would look funny if he started dumping stuff there while still clad in his protective clothing.

He checked with the Geiger on the wall and his own film badge. There was no radiation to worry about, so he stripped off his suit and put it away. Then he carried the wreckage outside and round to the bin, hoping no one would notice him. Next day, he would pretend he knew nothing about the missing piece of equipment; and, likely enough, the chemists would think someone had moved it to another lab.

He made two journeys and the broken glass was almost cleared away when footsteps sounded outside. He ducked behind a bench, hoping to escape notice. He didn't want to be caught now.

The door opened and two men came in.

'Safe enough here,' one said.

Peering round the bench, Martin saw a small, thin man with sharp features.

'Soon make it safe,' the other grunted; and Martin received a shock. The speaker was Henry Garside himself.

Martin had never spoken to the boss of Garside Enterprises, but had seen him from a distance and had no difficulty in recognizing his dark, saturnine features. He wondered why Garside had come to the laboratory and was filled with curiosity. He watched from a crouching position behind the bench.

Garside took a protective suit from the locker and handed it to the small man.

'Put this on,' he said.

They both donned protective clothing and Garside pressed the button that lit a sign outside the laboratory: DANGER — KEEP OUT. Martin shivered suddenly; if Garside was about to experiment with the pile . . .

He almost stepped from his hiding place, but fear of losing his job restrained him. Panic stabbed through him as Garside lifted the latch of the pile door and opened it. The Geiger on the wall began to chatter.

'No one will bother us now,' Garside said, his voice at once muffled and metallic through the hood over his head.

The small man laughed.

'Not for long anyway!'

Martin glanced at his film badge and was reassured when he saw that it still retained its bright silver sheen. Radiation would blacken it with time, but he was safe for the moment. He decided he would wait as long as he dare before revealing himself. Perhaps Garside would not be long in the laboratory.

Both men sat on stools, and the small man said: 'You've reached a decision?'

'Yes.' Garside's voice rumbled like thunder. 'I'm waiting no longer. Some fool in the government declared the new weapon too dangerous to use, and no one else had the guts to stand up and say that if we don't the other side will! So I'm going to force their hands.'

'You've a lot of money at stake.'

'Billions I've sunk into it — and the government promised a multi-billion pound order. Now they're holding out on me. Well, we'll see.'

Martin glanced at his film badge. Already the edge had taken an ominous discolouring. His skin began to itch — or was that his imagination?

Garside's heavy voice broke in on his thoughts. 'You know the plan — I'm going through with it.'

'It could mean war,' said the small man.

'So much the better! There will be more profit in it if war comes — much more.'

There was a short silence, then Garside said: 'Repeat your orders.'

'I collect two suitcases. They'll be lead-lined and each will contain one half of an atom bomb. I smuggle the cases into the capital and arrange it so the bomb is set off by remote control. Then clear out.'

'And the eastern alliance will take the

blame,' Garside added smugly. 'The government will panic, push through legislation to put the new weapon into production, and I'll collect a fat profit on the deal.'

Martin listened, horrified. It seemed incredible to him that two of his own countrymen could plan the cold-blooded murder of thousands of people for money. He had a sudden desire to leap out and denounce them, but fear held him back. He knew now that he would lose more than his job if he were discovered.

Worried, he glanced down at his film badge again. The blackness was spreading across the disc. And he must stay in hiding.

'The bomb is ready packed,' Garside said. 'The two cases are ready for clearance and you'll have no trouble getting them out. I will personally sign the necessary papers. You'll collect them at the main gate in exactly three hours from now.'

'It'll be dark then,' the small man grunted. 'I'll drive through the night to the capital. A couple of hours to arrange

139

the detonation, and I'll be away. Explosion twelve hours from now.'

'Fine,' said Henry Garside. 'Couldn't be better.'

They discussed details; the hotel room already prepared to receive the bomb; the agent's escape route; the foreign bank with which Garside would deposit an agreed sum of money immediately the government authorized production of the new weapon. They did not mention the thousands who would be killed and maimed because of their diabolical plan.

Finally, they left the building.

* * *

Frank Martin rose from his cramped position. His skin burned and he felt slightly sick; sweat ran down his cheeks. He looked once more at his film badge and froze in icy apprehension. *The circular disc was black as night.*

He ran outside and headed for the medical block. He ran between concrete walls where Geigers were fixed; and they chattered as he passed. A great fear gripped him and his heart pounded wildly.

He tore through the swing-doors of the medical section and startled men looked up at the sudden fury of their radioactive counters. They backed away and left him alone.

Abruptly, a warning bell added its peal to the noise of the Geigers and a decontamination squad surrounded him. Men in special suits, their hands inside metal claws, swooped and held him. He was carried to a table and a doctor used testing instruments on him. An orderly prepared a hypodermic syringe.

'Garside,' jerked out Frank Martin. 'Stop him. He's — '

The needle jabbed his arm and the racing thoughts surging through his brain tumbled into chaos. His lips babbled incoherence. Darkness gathered and he slid into oblivion.

★   ★   ★

He returned slowly to consciousness. It felt as if fire flowed through his veins and there was a void where his stomach should be. His head ached. He lifted a hand to his head and saw that it glowed . . .

'Garside,' he said, and sat up abruptly.

'Mr. Garside is safe,' a metallic voice assured him. 'Stop worrying about him.'

Martin saw the doctor and his orderly, both clad in protective suits. The Geiger had been muffled to deaden its noise but a red light shone above the door.

'Garside is planning to detonate an atom bomb in the capital,' he cried. 'You must stop him before it's too late.'

Under transparent hoods, the doctor and the orderly exchanged glances. There was a whispered consultation and another syringe prepared. The doctor's tone was soothing.

'You've received a bad dose, Martin. You're liable to imagine things. The best — '

'It's true,' Frank Martin interrupted violently. 'I heard it all. You must listen to me!'

'*You* listen to me, Martin. You've taken a fatal dose and there's nothing we can do for you. You have, perhaps, six hours to live. There must be someone you'll need to write to . . . use the time sensibly.'

Martin's hands shook as he clutched at the edge of the table for support.

'Six hours! Oh God . . . Ruth!'

'You'll want to write to your girl,' the doctor said. 'There's pen and paper on the table and I'll see that it is delivered.'

Martin moved to the desk, a vision of Ruth clear before him. He picked up the pen, and his hand wavered.

'Garside,' he said, and stopped.

The orderly came closer with the syringe.

'Best write that letter,' advised the doctor. 'Forget Mr. Garside. It's that, or we'll put you to sleep again.'

Frank Martin knew he had to do something to save the people Henry Garside planned to murder. He kicked the orderly's ankles from under him and ran for the door. The doctor, encumbered by heavy protective clothing, was too slow to stop him.

'Martin — stop!' he called as the door swung open. 'Think what you're doing.

Don't endanger the lives of other men!'

Martin ran out into evening shadows. He darted between high walls and kept moving. Behind him, the warning bell sounded again. His hands glowed with ghostly radiance and Geigers betrayed him. He could not hide for long; he must act, quickly.

How much time had passed? How long had he left? In three hours, Garside had said, the two suitcases would be waiting at the main gate. He must seize them and expose their contents — then he would be believed.

A man shouted at him to stop. He took another path and ducked behind an empty uranium container. Bulky figures with metal claws and radiation detectors were searching for him. He moved his position, heading towards the main gate. A voice boomed over the broadcasting speakers.

'We appeal to you to surrender, Martin. Your condition could be fatal to unprotected men. Do not risk contaminating others.'

Frank Martin shuddered. Why did it

have to be him? He didn't want to be a hero. All he wanted was to marry Ruth. It wasn't fair . . .

A figure appeared in front of him and light shone on the dark, saturnine features of Henry Garside. He was alone, and kept his distance for he wore no protective suit.

'You murderer,' Martin said bitterly. 'I'm going to stop you setting off that bomb. I heard you talking in the laboratory, planning.'

'You heard too much,' Garside said, and a gun showed in his hand.

Martin leapt back as the shot came. He turned and ran, and bullets kicked up the dust at his heels.

A searchlight cut through the darkness and revealed the bare white walls of a laboratory. The broadcast appeal continued. A decontamination squad hunted him . . . and Garside reloaded his gun and fired again.

He was close to the main gate now, running between Admin and No. 1 lab. He glimpsed the high wire fence marking the limits of the establishment and heard a tumult of shouting break out behind him. The whiplash of Garside's automatic drove him on. Then, rounding a corner, he saw the main gate and the two suitcases — and a small, thin man with sharp features.

Frank Martin hurled himself at the agent provocateur.

There was a glint of metal. Martin struck the gun aside and grappled with the small man, the momentum of his spring carrying them both to the ground. They fought; Martin trying to hold the agent; the small man struggling to get away.

It was like trying to hold an eel. The small man screamed and kicked and his features became distorted with terror. Martin clung on grimly, not realizing at first that it was himself who filled the agent with terror. He did not understand that he had only to keep hold of the man to kill him by his own radioactivity.

'Let go,' screamed the agent. 'For God's sake let go of me!'

He writhed and twisted and lashed out with feet and hands, panic turning him to a mad thing. He knew he could not last long in Martin's grip; he was fighting Death incarnate.

Martin had glowing hands about the small man's throat and was stopping the supply of air to his lungs. His wrists grew numb with the strain. He gasped:

'Tell them the truth. Tell them about Garside and I'll let you go.'

The agent provocateur began to babble a flow of words and Martin had to relax his grip so that others could hear. Men were coming up now and forming a circle about them.

'It's true,' wailed the small man. 'Garside planned to explode a bomb in the capital so the government would authorize his new scheme. He would have made billions out of it.'

'Out of the death of thousands of people,' Martin snapped.

'The bomb is in those two cases . . . let me go, damn you!'

Martin let his hands fall away and stood up. Nausea claimed him; he had saved a city but not himself. Six hours less how much? He felt suddenly weary.

Two men in protective suits took charge of the agent. Another started to open the suitcases, and government agents closed in on Henry Garside. Garside knew he had no chance now; he pushed the muzzle of his gun into his mouth and pulled the trigger.

Martin retched.

They were very kind to him, and assisted him back to the medical block. In other circumstances they might have shaken his hand, or kissed him on the cheek and pinned a medal to his chest. Instead, they left him alone to compose his last letter.

7

Grant In Aid

I had my feet up and a bottle tilted to my lips when the door opened and in walked a young man. He closed the door quickly behind him. He was nice-looking, blond, dressed in casuals, thick-soled shoes and rope tie.

'My name is Wilson,' he said, 'and I want to hire you.'

I lowered my feet and the bottle, spilled a package of cigarettes across the desk and motioned him to the visitors' chair.

'Fine,' I said. 'I need a retainer of three hundred bucks. Blackmail or divorce?'

He placed some money on the desk and I admired the crispness and design of it. It was a hot day. I had the window open and the blind down, and traffic sounds floated up to my office on the fifth floor.

'I want you to find out why a man named Lazarus is giving me money,' he said.

My thoughts stopped wandering. 'Say that again!'

'Lazarus has given me a hundred thousand dollars to continue my research into psi faculties. I want to know why.'

I released the blind so that it ran up and let the sunlight pour over his face. He blinked, but that was all.

'In my job,' I said, 'I hear some crazy things — but you *look* okay.'

'I'm as sane as the next man,' he admitted, 'but curious.'

I lit a cigarette and regarded him with steady concentration.

'Suppose you start from the beginning, Mr. Wilson . . . '

'Following the pioneering work of Dr. Rhine at Duke University, lots of institutions nowadays are interested in psi research,' Wilson said. 'I've been working at it myself, quite independently, for the last three years — and I've been aiming to take the whole business a step further. What I'm after is a *practical* application of psi.'

He paused, with an expression on his face that showed he expected me to be impressed. So I nodded.

'Three years,' he repeated. 'I was just beginning to get somewhere when my money ran out. It looked like I'd have to throw in my hand and find a job. Then I was tipped off about Lazarus — he might help if I showed him the results of my work.'

'Who tipped you off?' I asked.

'A friend of mine, Charlie Miller. He's been researching into hypnosis. Lazarus helped him with money when he needed it, so I wrote to Lazarus, enclosing my results and projected programme. I received one hundred thousand by return of post and no strings attached.'

'I'm in the wrong racket,' I said. 'I'd sure like to meet this Lazarus.'

'So would I,' Wilson said, staring me out.

'Mystery man, huh?'

Wilson nodded. 'He has an office on Wall Street. I went along there to express my thanks in person. I didn't get to see Lazarus — the man I saw called himself Tracey. He was small and old, cagey as hell — told me Lazarus never met anybody, that all communications went through him.'

Wilson pulled a sheet of paper from his pocket and passed it across the desk. 'I did some digging on my own account,' he said. 'This is a list of people, and the work they were engaged upon, who have received money from Lazarus.'

I read down the list:

Gordon — clairvoyance
Davis — Gestalt psychology
Zimmerman — author of *The African Medicine Man*
Hillier — psychomatics
Glinke — automatic writing
Dewer — author of *A New Valuation of the Spirit World*

Wilson said: 'I don't suppose the list is exhaustive. The interesting point is that all of us have been engaged upon work into what I might call, 'the science of the mind'.'

'Yeah, you might call it that,' I told him. 'This Lazarus has a bug about it and the money to indulge his whim. Rich guys are like that. It's legal — there's nothing to investigate. Why not pocket the dough and forget him?'

'I have a hunch there's more to it than that. Lazarus is encouraging research into the one field orthodox science has ignored, the field of human personality. Make no mistake about this, Mr. Stone, if we succeed in finding natural laws behind the minds of men, and applying those laws, then we've got something really big . . . bigger than nuclear physics, for instance.'

'Okay,' I said. 'I'll look into it if that will make you happy.'

After Wilson had left, I took the elevator down to street level, collected my auto and drove north to my apartment. The sun was blinding hot, there wasn't a breath of air stirring. I showered and changed into a dry shirt, ate at a drug store and drove towards Wall Street.

Tracey's office was small; just a desk, two chairs and a phone. Like Wilson said, he was small and old; retired lawyer would be my guess at his occupation.

I said: 'I'd like to fix an appointment

with Mr. Lazarus.'

Tracey didn't bat an eyelid.

'I regret that is impossible,' he said drily. 'Mr. Lazarus sees no one. If you will state your business, I will see that Mr. Lazarus is informed.'

He waited me out.

'I'm working on a new theory of telepathy,' I lied. 'I need money to continue my research.'

'Mr. Lazarus will be glad to help you. All you need do is prepare a synopsis of your theory and send it to this office. I will transmit it to Mr. Lazarus and he will make a grant depending on his valuation of your ideas.'

I seated myself on a corner of Tracey's desk and lit a cigarette.

'Look,' I said, 'all I want is to get to see your boss. Why the mystery?'

'Mr. Lazarus sees no one,' he repeated.

'Yeah, you said that. Now tell me what he looks like — *you* must have seen him.'

Tracey shook his head.

'I have never met Mr. Lazarus. All my business with him is done by mail.'

I looked close at him. He wasn't lying.

'Okay,' I said, 'I'll write — maybe.'

I dropped my private card on his desk and walked out, thinking Lazarus wouldn't want to pass up a chance to hand out dough. I was playing hard to get.

I checked with Charlie Miller and Dewer, the only two on Wilson's list who lived in New York. I learnt nothing. I tapped Tracey's phone, but the only calls he got were from people needing money. Tracey never once called Lazarus.

I checked on Tracey, too. He had a comfortable house and a bank account; he moved from his house to the office and back again. I tired of watching him.

Wilson called again and paid another three hundred bucks to keep the investigation open. I had one divorce case and Tracey wrote reminding me to send in a synopsis of my theory; Mr. Lazarus would be encouraging, he hinted.

It seemed the only thing to do was tamper with the U.S. mail. Accordingly, I waited one morning for the collection and passed the mailman five bucks. Sure enough, Lazarus had an address out of town and I drove out.

The countryside was a pleasant shade of green, the air clean and the highway practically deserted. I passed some pretty large houses set in county-sized grounds, walled off from the casual eye. If Lazarus lived in this style, the man I was dealing with was another Rockefeller.

Presently, I was all alone in the world, just me and the winding road and miles and miles of high, glass-topped wall. The house was set on a hill with a view commanding all approaches, and it became obvious I wasn't going to sneak up unobserved.

I reached the main gate and pulled up. There was a lodge beyond the gate, and a man came out to look me over.

'Open up,' I said breezily. 'Mr. Lazarus sent for me in a hurry.'

He looked at me steadily, like a man memorizing a face.

'You want something, Bud?' he said.

'Yeah, I want to see Lazarus.'

'Beat it,' he said. 'Skip. Take the air.' He returned to the lodge and left me the wrong side of a solid iron gate that might not have been opened for years.

I turned the car and drove back towards the city. I didn't go far, just far enough to pass out of view from the house. I parked under some trees and lit a cigarette and waited for darkness.

The sun set, the sky clouded, and the moon wouldn't rise for a couple of hours. I headed back on foot, carrying a rug from the car. When I reached the wall, I threw the rug so that it settled across the jagged glass. I took a short run and jumped.

Inside the wall, I moved quietly, heading by instinct for the house on the hill. I didn't hear anything, but a heavy body knocked me flat.

Sharp teeth nuzzled my throat and a fierce growling did something scary to the pit of my stomach. The beam of a flashlight hit me between the eyes.

'Let him go, Buster,' said a familiar voice.

A hundredweight of mastiff rose up and I started to breathe again.

'Friendly sort of animal,' I said in my best conversational manner.

'He won't hurt you unless I tell him to,'

said the hard-faced guard I had met earlier. 'Just walk ahead of me.' He held a .45 automatic in his hand.

Buster followed at my heels.

We reached the lodge by the main gate and a man waited for me. He was slim, neatly dressed, a man of superior intelligence to my guard.

'Mr. Lazarus?' I asked hopefully.

He shook his head. Fingers worked deftly through my pockets and discovered my license.

'Who are you working for, Mr. Stone?'

'My grandmother,' I said. 'She's a hundred and nine and has to support her widowed father.'

The slim man was not amused. He sighed, like a summer breeze over water.

'You're outside your territory,' he pointed out, 'and Mr. Lazarus is generous with his donations to the police orphans' fund.'

He didn't need to read me the score. The county cops wouldn't like me.

'Don't come back,' he said.

My guard walked me outside, unlocked the gate and turned me loose. Buster took a last hungry look as I walked away.

Two days later, I received a check for a hundred thousand dollars. I tore it up and mailed the pieces back to Tracey, then I went to see Wilson. He listened to my report with a troubled air.

'I don't like it,' he said. 'If we really discover a set of natural laws behind psi phenomena, it could be the biggest thing in the history of our race — and the biggest menace, in the wrong hands. Isn't there any way you can get into that house?'

I assured him there was.

Clint Stevens and I had served in the forces together. He'd do what I asked, and without questions. More important, he ran a small commercial airline and owned a helicopter.

It was a cloudy night with the moon showing faintly when I dangled at the end of a rope ladder. Below my feet, the roof of the house angled away. I hit a chimney stack, let go, and rolled to the edge of the parapet. Clint took the heli up and away and I was on my own.

I found a rain-pipe that led close to a

window, and the window wasn't barred. I used a jemmy to force the latch and climbed in. The room was empty. I padded across to the door and listened, opened it, moved into a long corridor.

I had a flashlight in one hand and a revolver in the other. This time I wasn't going to be stopped. The top floor was empty, with thick dust, so I moved down to the next floor. Nothing there, either. A light showed from a room on the ground floor and I crept towards it.

The slim man sat at a desk, writing. He looked up as I entered.

'I told Mr. Lazarus to expect you,' he said easily. 'You shouldn't have sent back the check, Mr. Stone.'

'I'm an honest man — '

I marched into the room with my revolver pointing at him. I didn't march far. Inside, there was a man either side of the door, big men. Without speaking, they each took one of my arms and lifted. My feet rose in the air and my gun hit the carpet.

Suspended, helpless, I watched the slim man rise from his seat. He opened a drawer of his desk and pulled out a hypodermic.

'This won't hurt,' he assured me. 'Just a little something to put you to sleep.'

I felt the prick and the curious pounding sensation of a liquid penetrating my veins. I felt heavy as lead and the room rippled in waves as seen through water. It got darker and darker and my last conscious thought was one of fear.

I woke to utter blackness in a room whose air was humid. I felt light-headed, relaxed. The room was small and the walls metal-hard to the touch. There didn't seem to be a door or any windows.

I hammered on part of the wall and let out a yell to indicate I was back in circulation.

A voice spoke, a voice with an oddly mechanical accent.

'I am Lazarus. You will not be harmed, Mr. Stone, but certain precautions must be taken. You are being moved to a place of safety.'

'New York suited me fine,' I assured him.

'You will not see New York again.'

'Kidnapping is a Federal offence. At least two people know I visited your house.'

'Your disappearance will be accounted for, Mr. Stone. It is not the first time I have had to resort to such means to hide my activities.'

'What's your game?' I challenged.

The answer never came, and after a time I tired of being ignored and started again to hammer on the walls. I kicked up a hell of a racket.

Lazarus spoke: 'Please stop wasting your energy.'

'Then show yourself,' I demanded.

After a pause, that strange voice said: 'I am all about you, Mr. Stone.'

I didn't like the implication behind that, and snarled: 'Who are you kidding? I'm out of the nursery . . . '

'Are you? Are any of your race?'

'*My* race!' I licked nervously at lips suddenly dry. 'What the hell are *you?*'

There was no answer. The silence went on and on, and my thoughts had nothing to fill it.

'Lazarus,' I whispered, 'are you trying to tell me you're not human?' Again I received no reply.

'What's all this about psi faculties?'

The darkness, the silence, was shredding my nerves. I began to shout.

'Damn you, answer me!'

Lazarus said: 'You must wait till you arrive where you are going.'

'Where's that?'

'A long way.' There was a pause, then: 'Have you never looked at the stars, Mr. Stone, and wondered whether the planets revolving about them are inhabited?'

'Sure,' I said. 'Where does that get us?'

He didn't answer and the long silence was back. I never met anyone so reluctant to talk as Lazarus. I began to kick the walls again; that seemed the one thing I could do to annoy him.

'Suppose, Mr. Stone, that the inhabitants of these other worlds are more advanced than your own race. Suppose that when you develop certain latent faculties you achieve maturity.'

'All right — suppose it,' I prompted.

But that was the end of another conversation. I tried to fit the pieces together . . . the human race had to rise by its own effort . . . the most Lazarus could do was remove material barriers.

He spoke then, as if aware of my thoughts.

'I am going to raise another barrier . . . '

I heard a metallic click. Then there was blinding light from outside, and a black void studded with stars. The moon seemed very much larger — only it wasn't the moon. It was blue-green in colour and I clearly recognized the contours of the American continent.

8

The Relic

The girl's high heels clacked through the silence of the empty street. Pale light filtered down, revealing apprehension in her face as she looked back over her shoulder. A high, unbroken wall of crumbling brick blocked her freedom on one side; a certain tenseness gave her the manner of a hunted animal.

Ahead of her, a shadow fell across the uneven paving, cutting across her path, a long and jaggedly sinister shadow. She stopped, pressed back against the wall, her breathing noisy. Her hands flew up to hide the terror in her face as the shadow crept steadily nearer. Her body strained in anticipation . . .

'Lights!'

The scene was immediately transformed as powerful studio lighting flooded the set, destroying the atmosphere and silhouetting a tangle of cables and the huddled camera crew.

Julie Lake relaxed, blinking as she groped for a cigarette.

Chan Carlos, no longer a threatening shadow, flicked his lighter and held it out to her.

Max Gribble, holding a bulky script, said: 'Get some fog into this scene. I want it swirling round her as Chan comes up. Wardrobe, take the vee of Julie's neckline lower. Props . . . where the hell's Props? We can start shooting as soon as Chan's fitted with his hump.'

A neat grey man stepped forward, holding a bulky object reverently in his hands. 'Here, Mr. Gribble. I didn't like to interrupt while you were rehearsing. I've got it, as I told you — the real one, I mean. The relic.'

Chan, veteran actor of a score of vampire-werewolf films, didn't recognize the man; then remembered their property-man was in hospital following an accident. He glanced distastefully at the hump and said:

'What's this about a relic?'

The grey man — he wore a grey suit that somehow seemed to neutralize his face — answered smoothly: 'I was telling Mr. Gribble earlier. I managed to track down the original hump, the one *he* used.'

Chan stared blankly. 'But he was a hunchback — anyway, he was lost in the fire.'

'No, Mr. Carlos,' the grey man corrected. 'No, I'm afraid that's another popular myth. He used a hump to disguise himself, and to frighten people, of course. It's strange how frightening a hunchback can be, just because his back's crooked ... but the Hunchback of Hammerhill wore this ... '

He held out the misshapen lumpy thing for inspection. Chan's nostrils wrinkled in distaste. Whatever it was, it was old and evil-smelling. He touched it, and his hand recoiled from something — clammy.

'I don't see why props can't make a new one — this isn't a low-budget job.'

'But this is the real hump,' the grey man wailed. 'I went to a lot of trouble to locate it.'

Gribble, the director, laughed cynically. 'I just bet it's the real one! Still, that'll make good publicity — go over big. Chan Carlos wearing the genuine hump used by the madman. Yeah, that'll pack 'em in.'

Julie Lake smiled warmly at Chan. 'I'd be ever so much more frightened of you, just knowing it was the real hump.'

He surrendered. A starlet with no acting ability, but how she turned him on. And at my age, he thought, infatuated by a pair of thighs . . .

'All right, Julie, to please you.'

'That's settled then,' Gribble said.

Chan followed the grey man back to the dressing room, past looming stage sets. 'What's your name?' he asked. 'How did you get hold of this thing?'

'Wyles, Mr. Carlos, that's me. And I heard of it through a friend of a friend — you know how it is in this business.'

Wyles closed the dressing room door. 'You'll have to remove your shirt, Mr. Carlos. It fits to the shoulder muscles by a sort of harness. You'll see, everyone will think you're a genuine hunchback.'

Chan viewed the relic with increasing distaste as he stripped to the waist. He turned, facing a litter of greasepaints on the dressing room table, suffered having the clammy thing fitted to him. Clammy? He seemed to have got his sensations mixed. Now it felt warm, seemed to pulse. He began to wriggle . . .

'Steady, Mr. Carlos,' Wyles murmured. 'Give it a moment.'

Chan stared into the dressing table mirror, turning to get a clearer view. There was no doubt that it moulded itself to his back, with no sign of a harness; it just appeared to cling there, of its own volition. He felt the oddest sensation, as though it were adjusting itself to his own personal contours.

A few minutes later, as he dressed, he was hardly conscious of the thing — it seemed relatively weightless. It became a part of him as he thought himself into his role, the Hunchback, murderer and maniac . . . he took a few shuffling steps.

'Perfect,' Wyles said, with something almost like enthusiasm. 'You're just right for it, Mr. Carlos. It fits you like a glove.'

Chan went out on the set.

Gribble nodded to him. 'All right, everybody, let's see how it goes. Take

One. Lights. Camera.'

It went well for Chan Carlos. Rarely had he got the feel of a new part so swiftly, so surely.

As Gribble called: 'Cut!' Julie looked strangely at him.

The director was enthusiastic. 'The best thing I've seen you do, Chan. Keep this up, and we've got the greatest box office since Dracula.'

Chan was pleased. But, back in his dressing room at the end of the first day's shooting, he felt uneasy as his hump was removed. He felt uncomfortable without it, as if he'd lost part of himself.

He drove to his flat, ate a light snack and poured himself a drink. He sat in an armchair to read through the old newspapers he'd collected from the time of the horror . . .

THE HUNCHBACK OF HAMMERHILL
Monster destroyed

The biggest manhunt since Jack the Ripper ended tonight. Since the shocking murders of five young girls in our city streets, police cordons have nightly sealed off the area in which the Hunchback operates. And tonight the madman was trapped — trapped and utterly destroyed in a mysterious fire that broke out in the warehouse in which he sought refuge.

Our streets are safe once again. Never more will a young girl feel terror as the Hunchback's shadow crosses her path. Never again will come the terrible discovery of a half-eaten corpse, where the maniac fed on human flesh till he was disturbed . . .

Chan Carlos undressed and went to bed. His back itched and he twisted to look in a mirror; he saw a row of tiny red dots. He spent a restless night, dozing fitfully to be woken by nightmares.

By morning, back in the studio with his hump fitted, he felt better.

The first scene went well, with no need for a retake, and Gribble was pleased as they broke for coffee.

Chan looked for Julie — for some reason she seemed to be avoiding him — and found her talking to Gribble. Her manner was unusually earnest.

'Max, he's too damned real in this part. He scares the pants off me.'

Gribble grinned. 'Good! This is a horror film, and I want you scared, Julie — really scared, not just acting. You keep in mind the hump Chan is wearing is the real McCoy, keep that right in front of your tiny little mind.'

Julie shuddered as she turned away.

'All right, let's get on with it. Positions, everybody.'

Chan, his feeling for the role developing uncannily, gave the best performance he'd ever given. He sensed this strongly, and Gribble confirmed his feeling. Julie's shocked white face merely added confirmation.

Chan began to wonder if it were really the hump the Hunchback had worn, and if it could be affecting him in some way.

After a few day's shooting, he refused to have the hump removed as they went off-set. Instead, he wore it home. He felt more comfortable somehow; the hump had really become part of him.

Gribble nodded casually when he mentioned it. 'Anything you say, Chan. You're going strong, and we don't want to risk spoiling your feel for the part.'

He wore the hump to bed, slept with it. He felt calm, the itching stopped and his tormenting dreams vanished. He was making an impression with this film, he knew; he hoped, eventually, to make an impression on Julie . . .

The following day, between shooting scenes, he looked for her. She was beside the coffee trolley. As he moved towards her, his shadow fell ahead of him, across Julie. She swung round as if stung — screamed and dropped her cup.

Gribble, alarmed, said: 'What the hell?' as Julie, white-faced, clung to him, trembling.

'Max, I can't take any more of this. Keep him away from me. He's not Chan any longer, he's not acting — he *is* the Hunchback!'

Laughing, Gribble detached her hands.

His voice was cool. 'Fine, that's just how I want it to be. You're giving out now, Julie. Really feeling the part, live on your nerves, that's the secret — we'll make an actress of you yet.' He paused. 'And I don't care what he does to you, understand? Just so long as my film's a good one.'

By the end of the next take, she was close to a breakdown.

Satisfied, Gribble dry-washed his hands. 'I've never known a picture go like this. No retakes. Every shot perfect. Hell, we'll be finished ahead of schedule at this rate.'

The camera crew sauntered away. The lights were switched off. Chan's eyes followed Julie back to the dressing rooms . . .

Julie Lake was late leaving. Her hands had seemed all thumbs as she changed. As she came out of the dressing room, she saw the darkened lot straight ahead, and shivered. She was alone as she turned abruptly into the passage leading to the exit.

The passage was narrow, dimly-lit, shadowy. Her high heels clacked through the silence, echoing the scene she'd

178

played so recently. Ahead of her, one of the shadows appeared to move.

She tried to calm the pounding of her heart. Nerves, she told herself, just nerves . . . there's nothing there. But she moved slower as the shadow lengthened.

My God, what a girl will do for money . . . She'd never take a part in a horror film again, never . . .

Then she knew, with ice-cold certainty, that the shadow was real that it was the shadow of the Hunchback, and fear paralyzed her.

She couldn't run. Her legs trembled as she pressed against the wall . . . just like the script, she thought hysterically. This was how he got them, scared, helpless . . .

Her body writhed, as it pressed harder against the wall. She knew what was coming . . . a hand touched her and she opened her mouth to scream.

The hand closed over her mouth, stopping her outcry. It pressed down, harder — and with the physical contact, her paralysis ended and she began to fight for her life. He was too strong for her. Her spine bent as he forced her backwards. Pain racked her. Chan, it couldn't be Chan . . .

The looming shape covering her appeared dark, almost formless. Air sighed from her lungs. Pain dulled as she slid down into unconsciousness. Killing her. He was really . . .

She had a moment of panic as the hump touched her before she blacked out.

* * *

Max Gribble, stepping from his office after pepping up a publicity handout, moved smartly towards the exit. This was going to be a great film, the greatest. He was going to be hailed as *the* director of Horror after this one. He knew it.

The passage was dark, shadowy and, as he heard, somewhere ahead, the sound of sobbing, he slowed his pace. There was something on the floor, an indistinct shape, bulky.

'Who's there?' he called. 'Is anything wrong?'

The sobbing continued. There was no

other answer. And now his nostrils twitched — whatever the smell was, it was highly unpleasant.

He groped for a wall switch, flooded the passage with light.

Chan Carlos knelt on the floor, tears trickling down his face. Before him lay the collapsed body of Julie and Gribble saw at once that she was dead. His heart stopped.

'Chan. You — '

Chan Carlos looked up, his jaw lax, his eyes vacant.

But even worse was the thing — the relic — it had detached itself from the actor's back. It was *alive*, moving slowly — like some bloated hedgehog — roving over Julie's body, feeding on her corpse.

9

Public Service

The city was high, wide and ugly; two hundred and fifty storeys high, crowding the entire length and breadth of the island, a teeming warren of inflammable miniflats. Somewhere in its humanity-congested structure a spark struck, hungry red tongues licked, a wall of flame exploded outward.

An alarm call went in to Fire Control headquarters.

From Control Sector H. Two-O a scarlet jet-copter shot up, whining expelled air, to direct the operation. Armoured hovertrucks, loaded down with fire-battle equipment, beetled out from the station yard, shrieking sirens clearing a path along traffic-jammed throughways that were hardly more than tunnels in the city honeycomb.

A few Inflams hurled abuse and missiles at the speeding trucks as they passed . . . 'Down with F.C.! Down with the Flaming Cinders!'

'Bennett's boyos again,' Section Officer Shane Riley commented as an empty plastican bounced off the safety glass of the cab. 'What the hell do they expect to gain?'

His driver, a scarlet torch on each shoulder tab of his smoke-grey uniform, laughed. 'Nut cases! They know they can't stop us.'

The truck hurtled on towards the heart of the conflagration, the unruffled voice of the Firemaster in the 'copter came down over the air-to-ground radio link: 'Phoenix One to all H. Two-O Salamanders. The fire is spreading fast through blocks seven thousand to seven thousand-nine . . .'

For a moment, Riley started. Jerry's flat was close to the danger area. Then he relaxed, smiling at the thought: Jerry wouldn't be home — he spent so much of his time at the Historical Institute it had become a joke . . . 'Why don't you move in and sleep there?'

The Firemaster's voice continued: 'Action to be taken — routine isolation.'

It was nothing but routine isolation these days, Riley thought, disgusted. And still Control barely coped with the outbreaks; with the island city growing yearly higher and even more densely populated, it was time to try something new. Anything. These were desperate times.

The Salamander truck raced along on its aircushion between towering walls, stopped at the intersection nearest the blaze and disgorged armour-clad men. Efficiently they unloaded their equipment and moved into action.

A mob — Bennett's Inflams again — harassed them and a struggle started up.

Watching, Riley snapped: 'Hoses!'

The operation went smoothly; jets from high-pressure hoses hit the mob, splitting their ranks and driving them back. Their howls of fury turned to frustration, were finally drowned out.

The firemen placed their charges. Fuses sparking, they turned and ran for the safety of the truck, climbed into the back. The door slammed.

'Task completed, sir,' the Sub-section

Leader reported.

Riley grunted acknowledgement, absorbed in watching a wall of red flame roar towards him, consuming block after block of miniflats; no matter how often he saw it, the sight still held a fascination for him. Eventually, a pall of smoke blotted the inferno from view, and he said: 'Take her out.'

His driver thrust one lever forward, jerked another back, and the truck turned in a tight arc. As they moved off, the explosive charges blasted, bringing untouched buildings crashing down around the fire area. Momentarily, the noise deadened the roar of the advancing flame-wall; then charges set off by other Salamanders went off in a maelstrom of sound that blotted it out completely.

The radio crackled to life again: 'Phoenix One calling. Spot-on timing — outbreak contained. Report back to Control Sector.'

A wide gulf had been blasted, encircling the fire to create a wind-break; and now powerful automatic pumps flooded the gap, pumping in millions of gallons of sea water to isolate the blaze, drowning like rats the horde of would-be evacuees fleeing death by burning.

Riley shivered, trying to close his ears to their screams, wondering how many thousands died this time? How many charred and waterlogged corpses would be buried beneath the new dwelling blocks? It was a recurring nightmare.

The fire isolated and left to burn itself out, the Salamander headed back to H. Two-O at cruising speed — a broad, heavy armoured vehicle riding an air-cushion. Riley saw — already! — the gigantic mechanized builders lumbering in like elephantine robots to rebuild on top of the devastated area.

No time was lost in re-housing the ever-increasing population of the over-crowded island city. More blocks of inflammable miniflats would arise . . .

Yet Fire Control was one never-ending battle, Riley reflected wearily. And they were losing the battle. Something else would have to be tried — but what?

The Salamanders grounded in the station yard; equipment was checked, explosive charges renewed ready for the next call. The jet-copter settled on the roof park.

Riley shot up in the express lift to the duty room to report.

The Firemaster, solid and grey-haired, a faint smile creasing his leathery face, had descended by the time Riley entered the long map-walled ops room.

'Nice job you did there, Shane — I knew you'd soon get into our routine.'

'Thank you, sir.' Riley had only recently been promoted to Section Officer. He was still on probation, still had to prove himself, so the Firemaster's words warmed him — though he wondered why he had been suddenly elevated over the heads of more experienced men.

The Firemaster said, 'Bennett tried it on again, I noticed. We'll have to fix that protest group of his — they're getting too damned impudent.'

The station officer looked up from his desk, waving the latest issue of a flimsy plastipaper. 'Have you seen this, sir? The *Union's* screaming for blood again — ours, of course.'

The *Union* was Bennett's news-sheet, mouthpiece of the Inflam party. Riley took the paper and scanned headlines:

FIRE CONTROL — MASS MURDERERS FOR FIREPROOFS!

How much longer must we be at the mercy of this so-called public service? Why are only the top people and their lackeys fireproofed? It is past time for a full-scale investigation into . . .

He frowned as he read on. It was dreary stuff, and he'd seen it all before.

'They don't seem to realize that if it wasn't for us the whole city would burn!' Riley's jaw hardened, his eyes smouldered; he didn't appreciate being called a lackey. 'Listen to this! Bennett's demanding nothing less than fireproofing for all miniflats; massive evacuation planning for all emergencies — '

The Firemaster cut in with a snort, 'Bennett's a double-dealer! The economy can't stand that, and he knows it. Traffic conditions forbid any evacuation. The man should be put out of the way, his party outlawed.'

'But something's got to be done,' Riley said, and bit on his tongue, wishing he'd kept silent as the Firemaster glowered at him.

'I'll talk to you alone, Shane.'

Riley followed him into the privacy of his office, a hallowed room decorated with Fire Control honours won by the Sector. The Firemaster sat heavily at his desk, polished bright, fingers drumming against the telecommunicator, watching him steadily.

'I hear you've been studying fiction, Shane — '

'History, sir.'

The Firemaster, a man who had come up through the ranks, continued as if he had not spoken. 'It won't do. You're a Section Officer and you have responsibilities. We're a realist service, have to be, and part of your job is to set an example. You should have lost this idealist taint by now. It's got to stop, or — you know what happens.'

Riley knew, and winced: down-graded to Inflam and the loss of his fireproofed miniflat. The threat was terrifying; his bones felt as if they'd been suddenly turned to liquid — yet he couldn't keep his mouth shut.

'Is it true, sir, that Fire Control once used to save lives? That water was used to put out fires, not just contain them? I know it sounds incredible but — '

The Firemaster's hackles rose. 'Heresy! Pure fiction. Remember your training course, the official records, it's all there, all you need to know. The city is everything, isolation our salvation.' He intoned from the *Fire Manual*:

'Fire Control means sacrifice, the sacrifice of the few for the many . . . anyway, you know these fiction tapes are banned, so get that stuff right out of your head. Forget Bennett's lies. Now — ' His voice toughened. 'I don't want to have to speak to you about this again. Dismiss.'

Worried, Riley went back through to the duty room, glancing at his chrono. The new shift was just coming on.

'Hi, Shane. Everything normal?'

'Yeah, routine stuff.'

Riley signed off, took a shower and changed out of uniform. His mood was uneasy as he left the station; it was his turn to visit Jerry — and he always felt uncomfortable in one of the Inflam blocks.

He rode a moving-way bridge across a canyon between city areas, dreaming a little. When his promotion was confirmed, he'd press his own ideas of fire prevention . . . now he had a chance to go to the top, perhaps even make Firemaster himself one day. That would mean a three-cell suite — fireproofed — and extra credit at the automat. He smiled briefly: it certainly paid to be a lackey.

Crossing from a Fireproof zone to Inflam, he flashed his pass at the checkpoint and escalated to Jerry's block, high above the city; here, the overcrowding was drastic and he felt hemmed in. There were no safety lanes in case of a fire-emergency and it took real effort to switch off his professional mind.

Jerry Drew lived in a cramped one-room cell at the very top of his block; and as Riley pressed the bell push he wondered again at their odd friendship. Contact between Fireproofs and Inflams was not illegal but, socially, anything more than a casual acquaintance rarely developed. Yet he and Jerry had felt drawn to each other from their first meeting — and not simply because they had a common interest in the history of Fire Control.

Jerry opened the door and Riley walked in, dropped into the window seat beside the rim-wall, looking out over the city and the close-jammed mass of Inflam blocks. It was evening, and a blaze of lighted windows killed the sunset, a milliard glowing oblongs reaching to every horizon. He sat silent, staring across the high towers, imagining every one of those lights as a potential fire. He shuddered.

'You're far away tonight,' Jerry said easily. 'Something on your mind?'

Riley looked back, aware of Jerry's scented deodorant; a new brand and overpowering. Perfumes became increasingly less subtle as population density soared.

He shrugged. 'Just the job, sometimes it gets on top of me.' He glanced at the scratch meal his friend had prepared; fishcakes and dehydrated vegetables, standard handout for the Inflams.

As they ate, sirens wailed. A fresh blaze flared up across the rooftops and lines tightened about Riley's mouth. His stomach refused to accept any more of the factory food. 'Another one! The situation gets worse every day. Something's got to change or . . . well, I just can't see how it'll end.'

He looked into Jerry's thin face, said, 'Why don't you let me try to get you into Fire Control? I'm sure I could swing it.'

Jerry smiled, shook his head. 'No thanks. I agree something's got to change, but not that way. Not just for me, but for all Inflams.'

Riley looked out to the distant fire, troubled. 'Perhaps you don't realize just how serious the situation is? It's hard enough for us to cope now — even sacrificing the few for the many — but with the population still increasing I don't dare think of the future. There must be other, better ways of control.'

'That's what Bennett says,' Jerry commented, amused. 'Maybe you two should get together — and you can, you know. There's a public meeting tomorrow, at Union Hall, and Bennett's speaking. No reason why you shouldn't go.'

No reason at all, Shane thought dryly, except the Firemaster wouldn't like it. 'I'll be on duty,' he said.

'Of course. Duty first, think later!'

Riley turned his back on the window. 'You know the answer, part of it anyway. Inflams have no sense of responsibility, nothing to do all day, and that makes them careless — careless with breeding habits, careless with fire. They bring it on themselves. There are just too many of them.'

'Is that from the handbook too?' Jerry asked mildly. 'It's time you started thinking for yourself — or let Bennett do it for you! Naturally, we Inflams have nothing to do now that all production is automated in underground factories. But that doesn't mean we're useless, with no right to live. We're human too!'

He waved his hand at the tiny cramped

living cell. 'Can you see me starting a family here?'

Riley said, 'The Fireproofs know what is best for the city.'

'The Fireproofs know what is best for themselves,' Jerry countered. 'The Fireproofs are the new establishment — you've seen some of my history tapes. The Inflam party and the *Union* represents the redundant — at least, that's how it started — at the moment I doubt if they represent anybody because the Fireproofs have the right of veto — '

'It's necessary,' Riley argued. 'What government could afford to take notice of the opposition?'

'A democratic one,' Jerry returned promptly. 'The sort of government we used to have before the fire service became Fire Control. *You* are the big whip the Fireproofs wield.'

'But that's history — before the Inflam blocks and the overcrowding. It was uneconomic to fireproof all cells.'

'History, remember that, Shane. History, not fiction.'

Riley sighed and lapsed into gloomy

silence. The evening was turning out to be less than satisfactory. He wanted to forget Fire Control, but couldn't rid himself of the feeling that a potentially explosive situation was about to detonate.

Sometimes he felt that Jerry was trying to involve him in something the Firemaster would not approve of . . .

After he left and rode back to his own fireproofed flat, he lay sleepless on his foam pad. In the early hours, his tormented brain slipped gradually into a dreamworld where monstrous rats ran before an avalanche of water, rats with human faces, and he heard the screams of the burning. He woke soaked in sweat.

When he reported for duty, there was a new order clipped to his In-file:

Bennett's protest group are holding a public rally at Union Hall to seek support for a change in Fire Control methods. Large crowds are expected. All sections will stand by.

More trouble, Riley thought sourly, initialing it. There always seemed to be trouble between Inflams and Fireproofs now. He supposed Jerry would be at the meeting, shrugged into his uniform with the torch tabs on each shoulder and joined his crew in the duty room.

'Salamander checked and ready to go, sir,' his Sub-section Leader reported.

Riley nodded and sat down at the table in the corner, dialed for a mug of instant-Bev. His crew matched tarot cards while they waited for a call, a sure sign of tension. The air-conditioner hummed louder, working harder to remove chemibac fumes.

Time dragged . . .

The alarm blared and the crew sprinted for the yard. As Riley came to his feet, studying the board — twelve thousand block, he noted mentally; God, that would be Union Hall! — the door of the Firemaster's office flung open.

'Shane! In here, fast!'

Riley hurried in, closing the door behind him, disturbed by this interruption in routine.

'Something special has come up. I'm giving it to you because it's kind of delicate. Come through and you're made. Fail and — ' The Firemaster made a chopping motion with one hand.

'I'll do my best, sir.'

The Firemaster paused, watching him. 'The situation has changed. You may have wondered why you were promoted . . . well, I knew you were friendly with the Inflam, Drew, and that he was one of Bennett's lieutenants. The idea was that you could keep an eye on them, but now — A fire-raiser has been trapped,' the Firemaster said quietly. 'The damn fool muffed the timing on his bomb when he tried for Bennett at Union Hall. He's caught in the blaze himself — and you're going to get him out!'

Riley stared back into the unsmiling leathery face, his brain whirling. The Firemaster had planned to use his friendship with Jerry . . . 'You mean, he *deliberately* — ?'

'Of course I mean deliberately. What else? It's time you grew up, Shane. How else do you suppose we keep the Inflam population down to a practical limit? City's way overcrowded as it is — without us, society would simply be impossible. It has to be done like this because it's the only way that works. Everything else we've tried has failed. So now you know what Fire Control really means . . .

'Only the top few in the establishment are in on it — and the Firemasters, of course. But this is an emergency. The fire-raiser — and that's his official status — is Comber, one of our best men. God knows how he got in this mess, but you've got to bring him out. Clear? Other Salamanders will isolate the fire — that's not your job this time. Get moving.'

It was on Riley's tongue to refuse, but he checked any outburst, knowing what would happen. Another Salamander would get the job, and he'd be downgraded to Inflam.

Knowing what he did now, that was unthinkable . . .

He walked stiff-legged, in shock, into the yard where his driver and crew waited, and climbed into the truck. 'Twelve thousand block,' he said, his voice steady; no one must guess how shaken he was. Routine, he thought; stick to routine, treat it just like any other outbreak.

The Salamander hurtled away, siren screaming, along one of the island-city's throughways. Riley sat in grim silence, seething, a pot on the boil. Why had he never suspected the truth? It was obvious now, all this emphasis on isolating a fire and leaving it to burn out . . . flooding the wind-break . . . 'sacrifice the few for the many' . . . 'there are just too many of them!'

Cold sweat oozed, gumming his uniform. Sick horror crouched like cramp in his stomach. He was on his way to save a fire-raiser, a man who cold-bloodedly caused uncounted deaths, leaving the innocent to burn. And what could he do except go through with it?

His driver stopped at the intersection before twelve thousand and looked questioningly at him. The crew were all expectant; they'd guessed something out of the ordinary was going on.

Peering through the cab window, Riley saw flames and smoke rise up to engulf whole blocks of miniflats — and somewhere in there, was Union Hall, and

Jerry. Was he even alive?

'I'll take her in alone,' he said dully. 'This is a special job. It means going to the heart of the blaze and one man can handle it. Move over, driver — crew bale out.'

His driver started to protest: 'Sir — '

'Orders! All out — and snap it up!'

As the last of his crew dropped through the hatch, Riley rammed the hovertruck forward, into a gap between burning buildings. Plasti-sheet walls crumpled, melting around him. Detonations blasted as other Salamanders built a fire-break. He was caught in a trap if his truck failed him now . . .

But it seemed he'd been living in a trap anyway. The Firemaster using him to get at Bennett. Had Jerry been using him too to spy on Fire Control?

Suddenly, he was ice-cool. The years of Fire Control training took over, torment ended, and he knew what he had to do: Get Comber out!

His radio carried the Firemaster's voice, steady as a rock, down to him: 'Phoenix One here, Shane. Comber's at the junction of twelve thousand and Gamma nine.'

Riley acknowledged, switched on his infrared searchlight and ploughed into smoke. He kept his attention rigidly on his routing, ignoring the violence of flaming wreckage, the screams of the dying. It was a nightmare trip into hell; the swirl of smoke, lit by greedy red tongues, the jumbled heaps of ruins to negotiate, the all-consuming roar of the fire, the secret horror locked in his mind.

He rode an aircushion through the Warren of Inflam cells, an eerie tunnel in the great city's honeycomb. The rendezvous point showed ahead, and a figure in asbestos suiting and smoke mask waved him down. He punched open the door and smoke came in, quickly followed by Comber.

Riley slammed the door again, worked his levers and turned the Salamander, heading back through the heat of the inferno. Extractors got rid of the last of the smoke from the cab. Beside him, the fire-raiser ripped off his mask to reveal a prim ascetic face, pursed lips, fair hair.

Comber coughed delicately. 'A nice

blaze,' he murmured. 'It should take care of Bennett for us. Glad to see you though — thought I'd cooked myself this time.'

It should take care of Bennett, and Jerry, and thousands of other Inflams . . . 'You've done it before then?' Riley heard his own voice, high-pitched, quavering.

Comber removed contact lenses, polished and replaced them. 'Plenty of times — after all it's my job. Inflam Control, we call it.'

Riley drove recklessly, teeth grinding. Inflam Control. Human beings murdered by the tens of thousands, incinerated, drowned. He felt sick. Comber filled him with such revulsion he could not look at him.

Through the cab window, orange flame sheeted . . . the result of Comber's firebomb. At an intersection just ahead, a party of men made a dash for it, trying to fight a way out on foot. They hadn't a hope . . .

As Riley approached, he instinctively slowed the truck.

Comber straightened in his seat, turning with alarm on his face. 'What are you doing? They're Inflams out there!'

But Riley was staring at one chalk-white face, a face he recognized. 'Jerry!' he exclaimed hoarsely, and stopped the truck.

The fire-raiser's gaze flickered out to the men, now running towards them. His voice lifted. 'That's Bennett there, and the whole point of the operation is to eliminate him. So you can't — '

'Shut up,' Riley snarled, and opened the cab door. 'I'm giving them a lift.'

Comber's hand came up sharply, bringing a gun with it, pointing it at Riley. 'Close the door and get moving,' he said coldly.

Riley shrank back in his seat, edging away . . . at least Jerry and Bennett were trying to change things . . . he heard a *psss* of compressed air, felt sharp stabbing pain in his shoulder. Anger surged through him; a terrible anger with the system, with the Firemaster for abetting it, and his anger focused on the man beside him.

He hurled himself at Comber, grappled with him, his strength increased ten-fold in his wrath. He was done with Fire Control . . . never again would he be a lackey . . . a bone splintered and Comber made an animal sound as the gun slipped from his grasp.

Berserk, Riley grimaced through a blood-red haze, lifting Comber bodily and hurling him from the truck.

That finished it, he thought; now he felt almost clean.

'Jerry,' he shouted, throat hoarse as smoke choked the cab. 'This way — hurry!'

A big man, broad and heavy, with a crag-hewn face filled the door of the cab. 'What's this game?' he demanded savagely, lifting a massive fist. 'What new devilry are you bastards up to?'

Jerry held on to the big man's arm. 'It's Shane, Bennett. Shane Riley, remember I told you about him.'

Bennett stared at Riley, grunting, then climbed into the seat beside him. Jerry and the rest of the party crammed into the back of the truck.

'Well,' Bennett repeated, 'what's the game?'

'Saving your neck,' Riley answered.

'And don't ask me why because I'm not sure, not sure of anything any more. Hold tight back there.'

He set the Salamander in motion, plunging into a new flame-wall.

The suspicion gradually faded from Bennett's face. 'So Jerry got through to you?'

Riley nodded, concentrating on finding a way out of the inferno. The ground shuddered, heaved, as twin towers collapsed and a bridge crashed down in a tangle of molten debris and showering sparks. Smoke billowed in clouds around the ruined stumps of buildings. Flames danced. It's *Gotterdammerung*, he thought dully.

He tried to blot from his mind the sight of charred bodies, bodies of men and women and children . . . fought down anger that threatened his reason. On and on he drove, the blaze seeming to stretch forever . . .

Then, abruptly, the Salamander jarred to a grinding halt. A towering mound of wreckage blocked their way, a mountainous heap that not even the hovertruck could surmount. Trapped! Riley felt desperate. They could not go back. It was forward — somehow — or perish.

'The end,' Bennett said coolly. 'But it was a nice try.'

'We're not done yet.' Riley's shoulder hurt like hell as he yanked the levers; he felt a driving need to survive, to fight back against a system that condemned men to a horrible death.

He turned the Salamander and zig-zagged back a few yards, felt her settle on uneven ground, tipped at an uncomfortable angle. He glanced into the back of the truck.

'Jerry — in the rack beside you — an explosive charge!'

Jerry passed him the charge and Riley set a short fuse and hurled it out.

They waited, tensed up, in gloom lit by hell-flares. Seconds dragged by. The blast could damage the truck, Riley thought, but it was this one chance or nothing.

The explosion came — a sheet of flame, a sound of thunder — rocking them, clearing a path ahead. A prayer on his lips, Riley gripped the levers and gave the powerful twin motors full throttle . . .

and raced through the gap.

'Where to?' he asked.

Bennett and Jerry exchanged a glance; Jerry nodded, and Bennett said: 'The Historical Institute. We've a secret place in the vaults that'll hide you and this vehicle. It'll serve us again.'

Jerry grinned. 'A rogue fire-truck!'

'Yeah,' Riley said, ripping the torch tabs from his uniform, 'We're all Inflams together now.'

He drove into steam, a great white cloud dense as fog as floodwater from the automatic pumps hit fierce heat. The Salamander began to rise, gently, riding the surge of floodwater. They were almost out of the devastation area, and he glimpsed one of the elephantine mechanized builders lumbering in to rebuild.

His radio screeched: 'Phoenix One calling! Shane — ' He switched off the Firemaster.

Bennett said: 'We'll have to fix your shoulder.' Then his voice hardened. 'Don't get any wrong ideas, mister — we're not fighting for abstract ideals, just plain survival. We've got a whole system to buck, and a lot of people are going to die before we change it. Maybe you, maybe me . . .

'But with a Fire Control officer with us — and you're the first to come over — there's a chance. There'll be others joining us now. You've given me our first real hope of winning.'

10

Cardillo's Shadow

Follow a shadow, it still flies you,
Seem to fly it, it will pursue . . .

— Ben Jonson (1572-1637):
The Forest

Mr. Cardillo was afraid of his own shadow. He did not, of course, tell anyone of his fear; that would have been tantamount to admitting mental instability, and Mr. Cardillo shuddered at the thought of confinement in a psychiatric ward. Nevertheless, his fear remained.

So nervous a man as Mr. Cardillo should not have lived alone in the old brownstone house on Cypress Hills. For one thing, the house had a bad reputation and was avoided by the local inhabitants; for another, it was too close to the cemetery to assuage his morbid fears. In appearance, Mr. Cardillo was thin and pale with a high forehead and watery blue eyes, and he habitually wore tight-fitting clothes of

215

faded black that exuded a faint musty odour.

He did not feel lonely, for he was a man given to solitude; he enjoyed the silent hours spent with his books in the dusty library — enjoyed, too, the feeling of companionship his shadow gave him. At high noon, it was an intense black blob very close to his heels, like a faithful hound; at evening, it stretched to a thin, flat counterpart of himself, faintly grey in the dim light.

Mr. Cardillo was on good terms with his shadow; it sat when he sat, walked when he walked, slept when he slept. Sometimes, Mr. Cardillo would bunch his fists and wiggle his fingers so that his shadow took on the form of some animal on the wall of his library; then he would talk to it, as solitary people will, first conjuring up a dream-image. Only Mr. Cardillo used his shadow. Like Mary's lamb, everywhere that Mr. Cardillo went his shadow was sure to go — until one day . . .

Mr. Cardillo was never quite certain when it was he first noticed the discrepancies in his shadow's behaviour.

For several days now he had been conscious of some slight irritation, without being able to place his finger on its exact cause. It seemed is if, from the corner of his eye, he caught his shadow indulging in a play of its own; yet when he looked, there was nothing unusual.

He dismissed the idea as fantasy, shrugging his thin shoulders — and was unduly relieved when his shadow shrugged in sympathy. Later, walking up the hill from the village, he noticed his shadow was blacker than normal for the time of day. It was almost as if it had gained in strength.

He stood quite still in the waning sunlight, staring down at the ground and the flat, black form reaching out from his feet. Instantly his shadow was still. Mr. Cardillo raised his free hand and wiggled his fingers; the shadow copied his movements, but without its usual instantaneous obedience. There was a time lag, as if it were reluctant to perform his bidding.

Uneasy in his mind, Mr. Cardillo dropped his arm and cried out in astonishment, for the arm of the shadow continued upward till the hand reached its face; there, the shadow placed a thumb to its nose and extended all four fingers in a gesture of ridicule and contempt.

Mr. Cardillo closed his eyes, opened them again to find the shadow copying his posture with meticulous care. He blinked; had he imagined that fantastic happening? He plodded onward up the hill, carefully watching his shadow for further signs of insubordination, but he reached the brownstone house without any recurrence of the abnormal.

That evening Mr. Cardillo became obsessed with the idea that his shadow played tricks on him when his back was turned. He paced the library carpet, apparently absorbed in thought; then he would whirl about in an attempt to catch his shadow in the act of some disrespectful gesture. He never succeeded, but the idea that his shadow enjoyed a life of its own persisted in his mind.

'Damnit,' said Mr. Cardillo aloud to himself, 'it's *my* shadow — it *must* do what I do!'

The idea that his shadow might not

always faithfully reproduce his own actions irritated Mr. Cardillo; he felt like a man whose wife is unfaithful. But he was not yet afraid — the fear did not begin until the next day . . .

Mr. Cardillo was in the habit of using a shortcut through the cemetery. The setting sun dropped a bloody shroud across bone-white tombstones, and the dark foliage of cypress trees shivered in a cool evening breeze, patterning the unweeded path with shifting shadows. An owl hooted its melancholy call from high up in the church tower.

Pursuing his course towards the brownstone house and the seclusion of its library, his conscious thoughts absorbed by the abstruse research paper he was engaged upon, Mr. Cardillo was alarmed to notice a slight but persistent tugging at his ankles. He glanced down, thinking to free himself of an entangling brier, and found nothing; he was standing in short grass and his legs were quite free of any encumbrance.

He frowned and walked on. The tugging at his ankles grew stronger as he approached a newly dug and yet-empty grave, the upturned clay wet and heavy and glistening. It was then he became aware that his shadow reached from his feet to the empty grave. With mounting horror, he conceived the idea that his shadow was trying to pull him into the pit.

He stood quite still, pale of face and heart beating faster, deliberately resisting the insistent tugging at his ankles. His shadow, long and flat and darker than it should be with some newfound strength, stretched out to merge with the intense blackness dropping away into the empty grave. It seemed, to Mr. Cardillo, there was something peculiarly obscene in the way his shadow strained against the fetters of his ankles, eagerly seeking to join its fellows in the world of darkness.

Terrified, Mr. Cardillo hurried past the open grave, dragging his reluctant shadow after him. His high forehead was damp with a cold sweat and his limbs trembled; he reached the front door of his house and fumbled in his pocket for the key. So badly did his hand shake that it was fully five minutes before he got the door open

— and, all the while, there was a frightful tugging at his ankles, urging him back to the newly-dug grave in the cemetery.

Mr. Cardillo slammed the door behind him, bolted and leaned against it, quivering with the weakness of a newborn kitten. When he reached the library, gone was all thought of a pleasant evening's research; he lit the lamp and surreptitiously studied his shadow.

He casually strolled the width of the room, watching the thin dark shape on the carpet; he sat down, crossed his legs; he raised his arm, lowered it. His shadow repeated the performance, this time without obvious reluctance. In fact, it seemed as if the shadow knew his thoughts, so quickly did it respond. It might almost have been burlesquing him, caricaturing his motions with devilish glee. Mr. Cardillo shuddered; there was now no doubt in his mind that his shadow had, in some uncanny way, become imbued with life — and that it was beginning to exert an influence over him.

Sleep was impossible. Mr. Cardillo lay on his bed, quaking with fear at the thought of the black shape beside him, a monstrous Siamese twin. He shuddered his way through the night hours to a tormented dawn.

It occurred to Mr. Cardillo that, perhaps, his was not the only shadow to rebel against its subordinate role in the scheme of things. For one terrible moment he had a vision of a world in which living shadows fought an unceasing battle with the material beings who gave them existence, a battle in which the shadows gained supremacy over the human race. Mr. Cardillo left the seclusion of his brownstone house for the bright sunlight of sanity with more than usual haste.

He spent the morning walking the streets of the village at the foot of the hill, maintaining a careful watch on the shadows of passers-by. Dark shapes danced on the cobblestones, simulating the actions of their human counterparts and, though he studied closely the fantasy of shadow-play, Mr. Cardillo was forced to acknowledge he could discern no discrepancies in the behaviour of these other shadows.

It was then, in the warm sunlight, that Mr. Cardillo began to have doubts of his mental balance. He must, he told himself, have imagined it all. He flinched, rejecting the obvious course of visiting a psychiatrist, and plodded back up the hill to the lonely brownstone house.

Mr. Cardillo paused, from time to time, to put his shadow through its paces — and on every occasion, it obeyed instantly and correctly. There was no hesitation, no hint of rebellion, so deferential to his slightest whim did the shadow appear, that Mr. Cardillo wondered if he had imagined its previous mockery of his actions.

He reached the gate leading through the cemetery, stood hesitating. He felt loath to pass that empty grave, even in daylight, as he remembered the dreadful tugging at his ankles, but he was tired, and the short-cut saved a further twenty minutes' walk. Surely he need fear nothing in the bright afternoon sunlight? Mr. Cardillo opened the gate and entered the cemetery.

Once be had closed the gate behind

him, the sun seemed to lose its reassuring warmth; a chill wind whispered through the cypress trees as he hurried along the path. Tombstones took on the ghastly aspect of yellowed molar stumps set in grim jaws, waiting to devour him.

Mr. Cardillo's feet moved with urgent speed, and his shadow danced before him, black and strong and eager. The newly dug grave with its pyramid of heavy clay loomed ahead; the shadow reached out dark arms, avidly seeking the cradle of its evil life.

Mr. Cardillo checked in mid-stride, ice-cold and stiffening with fear. Before his horrified eyes, the shadow writhed and stretched in a way that bore no resemblance to his own still and petrified form. The dark shape lengthened till its hands reached the edge of the grave; groping fingers crawled over the crumbling brink, secured a tenacious hold in the heavy clay soil.

There came a sudden, vicious jerking at Mr. Cardillo's ankles, and he felt himself being drawn steadily nearer the open pit. He dug in his heels, resisting his shadow's attempt to pull him towards the grave; he strained against the dark thing on the ground, shuddering at its hideous life. The branch of a tree brushed his face, and he grabbed it, his thin hands clutching the branch so tightly he bruised the skin over his knuckles. He held on grimly, fighting his shadow more desperately than any man ever fought a human enemy. Whether he could have won that terrible tug-of-war, Mr. Cardillo could not even guess; his shadow was far from exhausted when it released its hold on the edge of the grave. It snapped back at him, like a puppet on elastic, writhing in the cold bright sunlight, clawed hands reaching for his throat.

Stumbling in mad flight, Mr. Cardillo raced for his house, ran before his shadow as thin dark hands sought to choke the life from him. He crashed through briers and tangles of weeds, sobbing in terror, white-faced and trembling; he escaped the grinning tombstones and collapsed against the front door of his house.

The sun began to warm him again and, when he looked, his shadow was close at his heels, copying his gestures with open mockery, as if it knew its power was increasing and need no longer bother with the pretence of lifeless subordination. Mr. Cardillo went into his house and locked himself in.

Sunlight flooded through the library windows, and Mr. Cardillo's shadow flickered across the carpet, maliciously intent on its macabre play. It gave up the burlesque of his actions and eagerly explored the room, darting from corner to corner, climbing the walls, scuttling over dusty shelves, burrowing under furniture. Now it appeared more intensely black, more *solid*, than ever before; its vitality was frightening.

Mr. Cardillo shuttered the windows; but the light, filtering through cracks he had never before noticed, revealed the hideous thing as it roved at will. He drew heavy curtains, blocked the crack under the door with newspapers. The room was dark, the air still, the shadow no longer visible.

Mr. Cardillo sat in a chair in utter blackness, unseeing, yet knowing his shadow was ever present, a dark form hovering over him, following his every movement with uncanny prescience. Sweat froze in tiny beads on his pale face; his hands were clammy and trembling.

The hours passed, and Mr. Cardillo sat unmoving in his chair. His body felt weak, his eyes heavy with lack of sleep, his face lined with fear. The room was cold, and he knew the sun had gone down and it was night-black outside. Still he lit no lamp; he was afraid to see that flickering, effervescent thing which had once been his shadow. He knew it was still with him, could feel its aura of power grow stronger as he weakened, as if it were draining the life-force from him, feeding on him in some vampiric way.

He could feel it tugging at his ankles, trying to pull him out of the chair; it wanted to go out into the moonlight, back to the cemetery and the newly dug grave. The tugging was insistent; Mr. Cardillo could only keep his legs from moving by holding them down with his hands; his feet tapped an odd rhythm on the carpet

The very darkness became oppressive, seemed to close in about him, stifling him. A dreadful coldness saturated him, numbing his arms; his body stiffened and only his legs moved with restless urgency, forcing him upright, carrying him towards the door.

Mr. Cardillo wrestled with the lock, opened the door and went on to the porch. Silver-pale moonlight glittered on the cypress trees in the cemetery. His shadow ran eagerly forward, black and strong and full-bodied, dancing with wild abandon, revelling in the knowledge of its triumph. With shuddering hands and leaden face, Mr. Cardillo opened the gate of the cemetery and passed inside.

His shadow darted like an arrow for the empty grave — *and Mr. Cardillo followed* . . .

We do hope that you have enjoyed reading this large print book.

Did you know that all of our titles are available for purchase?

We publish a wide range of high quality large print books including:
Romances, Mysteries, Classics
General Fiction
Non Fiction and Westerns

Special interest titles available in large print are:
The Little Oxford Dictionary
Music Book, Song Book
Hymn Book, Service Book

Also available from us courtesy of Oxford University Press:
Young Readers' Dictionary
(large print edition)
Young Readers' Thesaurus
(large print edition)

For further information or a free brochure, please contact us at:
Ulverscroft Large Print Books Ltd.,
The Green, Bradgate Road, Anstey,
Leicester, LE7 7FU, England.
Tel: (00 44) **0116 236 4325**
Fax: (00 44) **0116 234 0205**

Other titles in the
Linford Mystery Library:

ONE MURDER AT A TIME

Richard A. Lupoff

They'd been an odd couple, brought together by a murder investigation and discovering that they had an amazing chemistry . . . Hobart Lindsey is a suburban, middle-class, conservative-minded claims adjuster and Marvia Plum is a tough city cop who has fought her way up from the street. But now the couple have split and gone their own ways, both pursuing a series of mysterious crimes. Then fate throws them together again, reuniting them at the scene of a lurid murder . . .

THE 'Q' SQUAD

Gerald Verner

An habitual criminal attempts to snatch Penelope Hayes' handbag, yet is apprehended and charged. Two months later, she's abducted and chloroformed — and again rescued by the police. This time her assailant escapes with her handbag. It seems that the wave of daring criminal gang robberies across London is somehow connected to Penelope's handbag — despite her denials that it contained anything of value. Then she disappears again — and the police have a murder investigation on their hands . . .

MR. BUDD INVESTIGATES

Gerald Verner

Provost Captain Slade Moran arrives from Fort Benson, Colorado, to investigate the disappearance of an army payroll and its military secret. A grim trail has taken him to the empty payroll coach and its murdered escort, with one soldier mysteriously missing. Moran is led to Moundville where he's confronted by desperate men plotting to steal a gold mine. Embroiled in double-cross and mayhem, Moran fears he will fail in his duty. Against all odds, can he succeed?

NEW CASES FOR DOCTOR MORELLE

Ernest Dudley

Young heiress Cynthia Mason lives with her violent stepfather, Samuel Kimber, the controller of her fortune — until she marries. So when she becomes engaged to Peter Lorrimer, she fears Kimber's reaction. Peter, due to call and take her away, talks to Kimber in his study. Meanwhile, Cynthia has tiptoed downstairs and gone — she's vanished without trace. Her friend Miss Frayle, secretary to the criminologist Dr. Morelle, tries to find her — and finds herself a target for murder!

THE EVIL BELOW

Richard A. Lupoff

'*Investigator seeks secretary, amanuensis, and general assistant. Applicant must exhibit courage, strength, willingness to take risks and explore the unknown . . .* ' In 1905, John O'Leary had newly arrived in San Francisco. Looking for work, he had answered the advert, little understanding what was required for the post — he'd try anything once. In America he found a world of excitement and danger . . . and working for Abraham Ben Zaccheus, San Francisco's most famous psychic detective, there was never a dull moment . . .